Felâtun Bey and Râkım Efendi

Middle East Literature in Translation

Michael Beard and Adnan Haydar, *Series Editors*

Other titles from Middle East Literature in Translation

All Faces but Mine: The Poetry of Samih Al-Qasim
  'Abdulwahid Lu'lu'a, trans.

Arabs and the Art of Storytelling: A Strange Familiarity
  Abdelfattah Kilito; Mbarek Sryfi and Eric Sellin, trans.

Chronicles of Majnun Layla and Selected Poems
  Qassim Haddad; Ferial Ghazoul and John Verlenden, trans.

The Desert: Or, The Life and Adventures of Jubair Wali al-Mammi
  Albert Memmi; Judith Roumani, trans.

Monarch of the Square: An Anthology of Muhammad Zafzaf's Short Stories
  Mbarek Sryfi and Roger Allen, trans.

My Torturess
  Bensalem Himmich; Roger Allen, trans.

The Perception of Meaning
  Hisham Bustani; Thoraya El-Rayyes, trans.

The Story of Joseph: A Fourteenth-Century Turkish Morality Play by Sheyyad Hamza
  Bill Hickman, trans.

Felâtun Bey
and
Râkım Efendi

AN OTTOMAN NOVEL
Ahmet Midhat Efendi

Translated from the Turkish by
Melih Levi *and* Monica M. Ringer

With an Afterword by A. Holly Shissler

Syracuse University Press

Syracuse University Press
Syracuse, New York 13244-5290

Originally published in Ottoman as *Felâtun Bey ile Râkım Efendi*
(Istanbul: Kirk Anbar Press, 1875).

∞ The paper used in this publication meets the minimum requirements
of the American National Standard for Information Sciences—Permanence
of Paper for Printed Library Materials, ANSI Z39.48-1992.

For a listing of books published and distributed by Syracuse University Press,
visit www.SyracuseUniversityPress.syr.edu.

ISBN: 978-0-8156-1064-9 (paperback)   978-0-8156-5363-9 (e-book)

Library of Congress Cataloging-in-Publication Data
Names: Ahmet Mithat, 1844–1912, author. | Levi, Melih, translator. | Ringer,
    Monica M., 1965– translator.
Title: Felâtun Bey and Râkım Efendi : an Ottoman novel / Ahmet Midhat Efendi ;
    translated from the Turkish by Melih Levi and Monica M. Ringer ; with an
    afterword by A. Holly Shissler.
Other titles: Felâtun Bey ile Râkım Efendi. English
Description: Syracuse : Syracuse University Press, 2016. | Series: Middle East
    literature in translation
Identifiers: LCCN 2015045852| ISBN 9780815610649 (pbk. : alk. paper) |
    ISBN 9780815653639 (e-book)
Classification: LCC PL248.A3173 F413 2016 | DDC 891/.5532—dc23
LC record available at http://lccn.loc.gov/2015045852

for Roza and Estella

If we try to Europeanize only for the sake of becoming European, we shall lose our own character. If we, on the other hand, add the European civilization to our own character, we shall not only preserve, perpetuate, and maintain our character but also fortify and refine it.
—Ahmet Midhat Efendi, *Tarik* (1898)

Contents

Illustrations

Note on Translation

AHMET MIDHAT'S writing style in *Felâtun Bey and Râkım Efendi* is both charming and complex. As one of the earliest consciously modern experimental Turkish writers, Ahmet Midhat moved rapidly between Ottoman conventions and newer forms of language, syntax, and narration influenced by contemporary French and British novels. Ahmet Midhat was one of the first Turkish authors to punctuate the narrative with his authorial voice, inviting the readers to pause, to put down the text, and to pass judgments on the characters alongside him. At times the tone is playful and informal, even theatrical. At other times the tone is didactic and more complex with sentences that can run for half a page and clearly belong to an older elaborate courtly style influenced by Ottoman's intimate relationships with Turkish, Arabic, and Persian.

As translators, we juggled two objectives: to accurately convey the multiplicity of the text's styles, tones, and languages, and to render it readable by a contemporary audience. We strove to preserve even the deliberate repetition and occasional awkwardness of the syntax. Ahmet Midhat's fondness for idiomatic and metaphorical constructions necessitated an extensive search for comparable idioms in English that would have been in use during the nineteenth century.

Accurately translating times of day was problematic. In Ahmet Midhat's Ottoman Empire, people calculated time in relationship to the call to prayer, which is pegged on the position of the sun. Since sunrise, midday, and sunset in turn depend on the number of hours of daylight in any given day, it was very difficult to convey the equivalent of "two hours before evening prayer" with any chronometric specificity. Ultimately, there is no way to translate traditional times of day into a contemporary time frame.

We based this translation primarily on the original Ottoman text in its variant of Arabic script. The Ottoman text provided insights into the original structure and punctuation as well as Ahmet Midhat's usage of the Arabic and Latin alphabets. We retained the Arabic letters in one instance when they are being taught in the novel so that our readers would understand "the lesson." Similarly, we opted not to translate *Bey* and *Efendi*, two terms akin to "sir" and "mister," but with specifically Ottoman nuances suggesting the level and sort of education possessed by the bearer. Likewise, we retained the names of the Ottoman monetary units as *lira* and *kuruş* (1/100 of a lira).

The Persian poetry—both in the transliterated Ottoman spelling, and in Ahmet Midhat's "translation" of it by way of the principle character, Râkım—posed certain difficulties. First, the Ottoman spelling is not equivalent to the Persian. Second, while the poetry all purports to be by the Persian poet Hafez, several of the poems were misattributed to him—a not uncommon nineteenth-century error—and a misattribution that Ahmet Midhat himself was likely unaware of. Lastly, the main character Râkım loosely (mis)translates this poetry for his English pupils, making it all the more difficult to recover the original Persian. We are deeply grateful to Professor Franklin Lewis, who was able to translate the Persian poetry based on its misspelled and deliberately mistranslated version. Without his particular expertise, this would have been an insurmountable task.

Ahmet Midhat uses French words liberally and most often transliterates them into Ottoman script. However, when the two principal French characters (Pauline and Josephine) speak in French, he renders their words into the Latin alphabet and provides his translation in parenthesis for his readers. We retained all of his parenthetical translations from the French. The inclusion of French written in Roman letters was clearly a challenge for the typesetters of the Ottoman text, and there is one instance when the word "blonde" is mistyped variously as "dlonde," "blonde," and "londeb."

In keeping with his translation and synthesis of Ottoman and French language, culture, and literary styles, Ahmet Midhat frequently employs two hybrid words that are integral to the vocabulary of nineteenth-century Tanzimat reform: *alafranga* and *alaturka*. The term *alafranga* is a French-Ottoman composite of the French "à la" and "franga," meaning "Frank" or "European" more generally. *Alafranga* thus means "in a European mode." The term *alaturka* follows the same French-Ottoman composite pattern and conversely means "in a Turkish or Ottoman mode."

The aforementioned challenges of translating this work are symptomatic of an era that was itself undergoing a process of translation. As a result, the very question of translatability becomes a statement with concrete political implications. We hope that our translation preserves the immediacy of Ahmet Midhat's own position and brings to life the larger relevance of the cultural and literary debates of his time.

Acknowledgments

ANY STORY OF BEGINNINGS is inherently recreated—a reconstructed memory with the benefit of hindsight and therefore a distortion of the wealth of possible alternatives and dead ends. Certainly this translation is more the product of gradual evolution than of determined intent. We began reading nineteenth-century Ottoman literature as a way of investigating the literary manifestations of this quintessentially Ottoman exploration of "the modern." The cultural, political, and literary wealth of this literature compelled us to undertake a project that took shape first as a very rough translation simply to provide Amherst College students in Professor Ringer's history courses a window through which they could look onto this period. Their enthusiasm, and ours, propelled this project to take on the more serious enterprise of translating this translation—of not simply reproducing it, but translating it for a contemporary general audience. We like to think of this final version of *Felâtun Bey and Râkım Efendi* as a memento of our four years of conversations about nineteenth-century translation in all its various forms.

We are very grateful to Axel Schupf for his generosity. Without the intellectual and financial support of his invaluable fund at Amherst College, this project would have been inconceivable. Dean Ben Lieber's office also provided initial summer funding, which launched this project. Over the years, we have received substantial financial support from Amherst College's Deans of Faculty, Greg Call and Catherine Epstein. Rhea Cabin in the History Department never hesitated to offer a hand.

This book has been published with the support of the Ministry of Culture and Tourism of Turkey in the framework of TEDA Program.

We were fortunate to have had the opportunity to work with Michael Beard, series editor at Syracuse University Press, and are especially grateful for his thoughtful and meticulous recommendations, and most importantly, the enjoyment he took in this work. Anonymous outside readers provided painstaking recommendations for improvement. We, and our readers, have them to thank for this. Appreciation is also due to Suzanne Guiod, editor-in-chief of Syracuse University Press, for shepherding this translation to completion. The Atatürk Kitaplığı in Istanbul kindly provided us with the Ottoman publication of the novel from 1875.

Over the years, several conversations with scholars of Ottoman history and literature stand out as transformative. We are grateful to Nüket Esen, the leading scholar on Ahmet Midhat, for her insights. This project allowed us the privilege of having an unforgettable conversation on translation and Turkish literature with one of the most important scholars and translators of Turkish literature, Talat Sait Halman, whose encouragement was one of the most important sources of motivation. We were honored to have the chance to speak with Ahmet Midhat Efendi's grand-granddaughter Mutlu Tanberk, who didn't hesitate to share documents related to Ahmet Midhat, and allowed us the experience of getting to know him on a different level. At the very outset of this project we enjoyed a conversation with Professor A. Holly Shissler in the Ara Café in Istanbul, which was a memorable turning point in the development of this enterprise. Professor Franklin Lewis graciously undertook the translations of the Persian poetry. Rana Irmak Aksoy transformed the novel visually with her lovely maps. Heartfelt thanks to all.

Melih: I would like to acknowledge all of my professors at Amherst College for their invaluable friendship and insights. In particular, I owe special debt to Professor Judith Frank, who made the novel come alive for me, and to Ayşe Hillhouse of Üsküdar American Academy for igniting my passion for Ottoman literature. It goes without saying that had my family not encouraged me to pursue English literature at Amherst College, none of this would have been possible. And as for my parents, I couldn't have been luckier.

Monica: A special thank you to Ayşe Polat of the University of Chicago for all the hours she graciously spent teaching me to read Ottoman. And to Soraya, who always shares my endeavors.

Chronology of
Ahmet Midhat Efendi in
the Context of Ottoman Reform

1839 Sultan Abdülmecid I (r. 1839–1861) accedes to the throne, continuing the goals of his reform-minded father, Sultan Mahmud II (r. 1808–1839).

1839–71 Tanzimat reforms are inaugurated by the Imperial Edict of Gülhane (1939), which begin to break down legal distinctions based on religion according to Islamic law, seeking to make all Ottoman subjects equal under the law. The reforms continue as articulated by prime ministers Mehmet Emin Ali Pasha (1815–1871), Fuat Pasha (1815–1869), and later Midhat Pasha (1822–1883) as a means of strengthening the empire and protecting it from European imperial aggression. These efforts include measures to "modernize," centralize, and reform the government administration.

1844 Ahmet Midhat is born into a lower-middle-class family of artisans in the Tophane neighborhood of Istanbul.

1846 The Darülfünun, the first European-inspired modern secondary school, which later became Istanbul University, is established in Istanbul.

1847 The banning of the slave trade in the Persian Gulf by the Ottoman Empire marks the beginning of the movement for the suppression of the slave trade in the Ottoman Empire.

1853–56 The Crimean War.

1856   The Ottoman Reform Edict (*Hatt-ı Hümâyûn*) drafted by Ali Pasha is issued, renewing calls for legal equality amongst all Ottoman subjects, regardless of religion.

1857   Ahmet Midhat works as an apprentice in Istanbul's Egyptian Bazaar to support his family. In his free time, he learns to read and write from a shopkeeper in the bazaar.

1861   Sultan Abdülaziz I accedes the throne.

1861   Ahmet Midhat moves to Niš in Ottoman Serbia where he comes to the attention of Midhat Pasha, the leading architect of the Tanzimat reforms, who becomes his political mentor and gives Ahmet his own name, "Midhat," in 1865.

1863   The Ottoman Central Bank is established.

1864   Ahmet Midhat moves with Midhat Pasha to Ottoman Bulgaria to work as a government clerk. He becomes fluent in French and acquires his renowned familiarity with European literature. He also receives traditional training in Arabic and Persian languages and literary traditions.

1866   Ahmet Midhat marries Servet Hanım in Sophia, Ottoman Bulgaria.

1867   Namık Kemal (1840–1888), a Young Ottoman reformist and literati, is exiled to Paris.

1868   Namık Kemal begins publishing the journal *Hürriyet* (Liberty).

1868   Ahmet Midhat begins publishing articles in the officially sponsored newspaper of the Danubian province.

1869   Ahmet Midhat moves to Baghdad in the service of his mentor Midhat Pasha, who had taken up the position as governor. While in Baghdad, Ahmet Midhat edits and manages the official provincial newspaper there. He also meets Osman Hamdi Bey (1842–1910), the famous intellectual, statesman and Paris-trained painter.

1870   Ahmet Midhat publishes *Felsefe-i Zenan* (The Philosophy of Women).

1871   Ahmet Midhat returns to Istanbul where he writes for numerous newspapers, establishes his own printing press, and begins printing books at home in order to support his family. He soon makes the acquaintance of members of the Young Ottomans, a political group that criticizes Tanzimat reforms for their conservatism and advocates more rapid and far-reaching reforms.

1872   Ahmet Midhat moves to the Beyoğlu neighborhood of Istanbul.

1873   Ahmet Midhat is exiled to Rhodes along with members of the Young Ottomans, including Namık Kemal, as a result of Sultan Abdülaziz's displeasure with the political content in his newspapers.

1875   Ahmet Midhat publishes *Felâtun Bey and Râkım Efendi*.

1876   Sultan Abdülhamid II accedes the throne replacing Abdülaziz. The new sultan agrees to the promulgation of the first Ottoman Constitution; he also proclaims a political amnesty and Ahmet Midhat returns to Istanbul.

1876   Ahmet Midhat publishes *Paris'te Bir Türk* (A Turk in Paris).

1877–78 At the request of Sultan Abdülhamid II, Ahmet Midhat writes a book on necessary political, social, and economic reforms entitled *Üss-i İnkilap* (Basis of Reform).

1878   Ahmet Midhat becomes the head of the first official newspaper of the Ottoman Empire, *Takvim-i Vekayi* (The Calendar of Events). With the confidence of the sultan, Ahmet Midhat establishes and edits the most influential and longest running Ottoman newspaper of the era, *Tercüman-i Hakikat* (Translation of Truth) (1878–1922), which serves as a training ground for a new generation of journalists and writers.

1881   Ahmet Midhat publishes *Henüz On Yedi Yaşında* (Only Seventeen).

1884   Ahmet Midhat takes a second wife, Melek Hanım.

1889   Ahmet Midhat represents the Ottoman state at the Eighth Congress of Orientalists in Stockholm. While there, he makes the acquaintance of a Russian noblewoman and orientalist, Madame Gülnar (Olga de Lebedef), who later spent time in Istanbul. As part of his trip, Ahmet Midhat tours Europe extensively for two and a half months, visiting Germany, France, Belgium, Sweden, Norway, Denmark, Switzerland, and Austria.

1894   Ahmet Midhat publishes *Hayal ve Hakikat* (Dream and Truth) coauthored with Fatma Aliye (1862–1936), considered the first female novelist in Turkish literature.

1908   The Ottoman Constitution, which had been largely ignored by the sultan, is restored and Sultan Abdülhamid II abdicates the throne. Mehmed V (r. 1909–1918) becomes the thirty-fifth Ottoman sultan.

1912   Ahmet Midhat dies in Istanbul.

1914–18   World War I.

1919–23   The Turkish War of Independence.

1920   The Turkish Grand National Assembly was established in Ankara.

1920   The Treaty of Sèvres is imposed on the Ottoman Empire and the empire is divided amongst Western powers.

1922   The Ottoman Sultanate is abolished.

1923   The Treaty of Lausanne supersedes the Treaty of Sèvres and the Republic of Turkey is recognized internationally.

1924   The Ottoman Caliphate is abolished.

1924   The Ottoman Sultanate and Caliphate are abolished and Turkey becomes a secular republic under the presidency of Mustafa Kemal Atatürk.

1. *A Reader's Map of Istanbul.* Illustrated by Rana Irmak Aksoy.

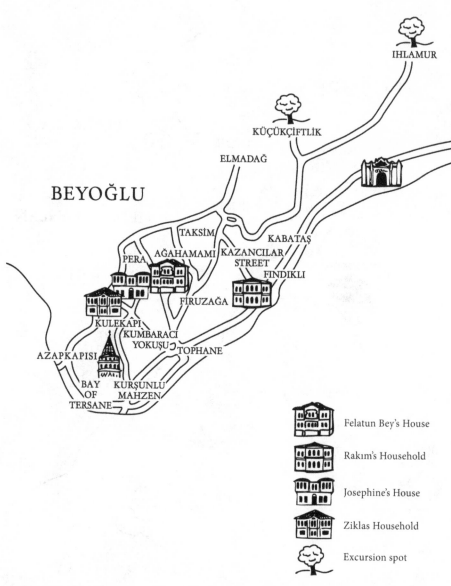

IHLAMUR

KÜÇÜKÇİFTLİK

ELMADAĞ

BEYOĞLU

TAKSİM

KABATAŞ

PERA   AĞAHAMAMI   KAZANCILAR
STREET

FINDIKLI

FİRUZAĞA

KULEKAPI

KUMBARACI
YOKUŞU   TOPHANE

AZAPKAPISI

BAY   KURŞUNLU
OF   MAHZEN
TERSANE

Felatun Bey's House

Rakım's Household

Josephine's House

Ziklas Household

Excursion spot

2. *A Reader's Map of Beyoğlu.* Illustrated by Rana Irmak Aksoy.

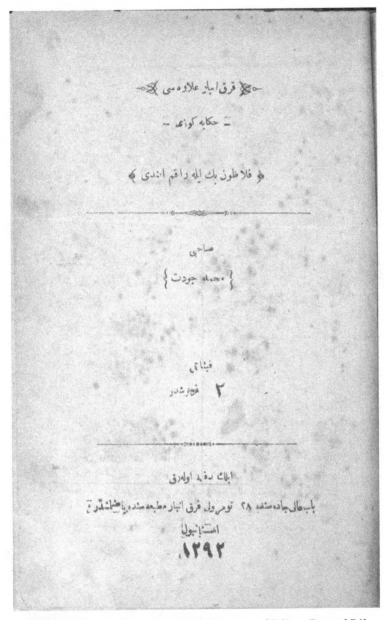

3. The front page from the Ottoman publication of *Felâtun Bey and Râkım Efendi*. Published in 1875 by Mehmet Cevdet. Provided by the Atatürk Kitaplığı (Taksim, Istanbul).

Felâtun Bey and Râkım Efendi

Chapter 1

HAVE YOU HEARD of Felâtun Bey? You know who I'm talking about, old Mustafa Meraki Efendi's son! Doesn't ring a bell? Well now, he's a lad worth meeting.

Mustafa Meraki Efendi lives in a district near Beyoğlu, in the Tophane neighborhood. There is no need to provide the name of this district. You know the neighborhood, right? Well, that's all you need to know.

He is a man of forty-five. If only, his father thought, if only they could get him married at a young age when he was still innocent and didn't know about the birds and the bees, he'd be able to preserve his honor and his manners. With this in mind, his father got Mustafa Meraki Efendi married when he was sixteen. That's why, although Mustafa Meraki Efendi is only forty-five, he has a son who is already twenty-seven: Felâtun Bey. And that's not Mustafa Meraki Efendi's only child. He also has a daughter, Mihriban Hanım. Now, at this point in our story, Mustafa Meraki Efendi is forty-five and his daughter is fifteen.

How splendid for a man of forty-five to have a twenty-seven-year-old son and a fifteen-year-old daughter. But let us remind you, this kind of happiness is reserved for fathers; as for mothers, this brings more trouble than happiness. And this was precisely the case for Mustafa Meraki Efendi's wife. For she was only twelve years old when Mustafa Meraki Efendi's father got them married. That's the way it is! The wife is supposed to be a few years younger than the husband! This twelve-year-old bride gave birth to Felâtun when she was fifteen. But after that every other pregnancy ended in miscarriage. The doctors couldn't identify the problem, so they gave up, saying that she had an incurable defect. Finally, the midwives, in their usual way, ended up delivering Mihriban Hanım. But her poor mother passed away while giving birth to her.

May God rest her soul! These things happen . . . What else can we say? With a thirteen-year-old boy and an infant girl in tow, Mustafa Meraki Efendi couldn't find another woman to marry after his wife's death. But after remaining single for some time, Mustafa Meraki Efendi didn't really see it necessary to get married since the last century's social progress in Istanbul now allows a man to lead a single life: he simply got a slave to serve as a nanny to his daughter and take care of the children, hired an elderly Greek lady to manage the household, and found an Armenian lady to cook.

How about that? Do you find the domestic arrangements of his home a bit odd? Our Mustafa Meraki Efendi was a man with an *alafranga* spirit. And do you know what sort of *alafranga* spirit? Remember the *alafrangas* of Istanbul from fifteen or twenty years ago? That's right, he was one of them. He was prosperous, very prosperous indeed, and possessed a beautiful mansion and an orchard in Üsküdar, but he nonetheless sold them off with no regard to price and had a pleasant house built near Beyoğlu, in Tophane, solely in order to live *alafranga*—that is, comfortably. Do you want to know how badly he wanted to live this *alafranga* life? Just look at his house! It was built of stone for that very reason: to be perfectly *alafranga*. Now, in a neighborhood and house of this kind, would such an *alafranga* man fill his house with uncouth Arab servants? Especially since his *alafranga* friends visited from time to time, Greek and Armenian servants were obviously necessary.

Because our main purpose is to acquaint our readers with Felâtun Bey, don't think it unnecessary to give information about his father's past. How can you understand Felâtun Bey properly if you don't know where he comes from? Surely, it's easier to understand someone's temperament and manners if you understand their roots.

We don't need to give long accounts of Felâtun Bey's childhood. As for Mustafa Meraki Efendi, who suddenly leapt from an extreme *alaturka* lifestyle to an extreme *alafranga* one, a change he sought in order to further material and spiritual pleasures, one can easily guess the kind of upbringing he provided his motherless son. By the time his son entered middle school, he was parading around with a school bag all day. He also had a French tutor who would come and go twice a week. Mustafa Meraki Efendi, who was not a very educated man and didn't take much of an interest in his son's education, thought middle school and a French tutor perfectly sufficient for a child's upbringing.

By looking at the kind of education his son received, you can imagine what his daughter's education was like.

However, let's admit that the way he dressed his children was above reproach. Whenever a new dress style became fashionable in Beyoğlu, Meraki Efendi felt obliged to be among the first to have his children wear it.

Ah! See, we almost forgot to tell you. The name of our Mustafa Meraki Efendi was actually just Mustafa Efendi. People started calling him "Meraki" "the curious" because of some odd behavior on his part. To give you an example, even though he could enjoy a magnificent dinner at home, some evenings he would stop at a grocery in Beyoğlu and buy olives and dried fish for dinner. When his friends criticized him, he would say, "What can I do! I can't help my curiosity!" And when people wondered why, rather than going to Naum's theater, he went to places in Elmadağı where the likes of fishermen and bird fanciers frequented, he would reply, "It's just curiosity," "I'm curious, that's all," and "I need to satisfy my curiosity." This is how he came to be nicknamed "Meraki" "the curious."

What we have recounted up to this point about Felâtun Bey is enough to give some idea of his past. Now let us return our gaze to the present, when Mustafa Meraki Efendi was forty-five, his son Felâtun Bey twenty-seven, and his daughter Mihriban Hanım only fifteen.

At this time, Felâtun Bey was a clerk at one of the government offices. Now, you know those gentlemen who, rather than working day and night on their own tasks, spend all their time inquiring into other departments' affairs in order to maneuver themselves into important state positions. You know the sorts of studious individuals I'm talking about . . . Well, our Felâtun Bey wasn't one of them. Why should he be? As the only son of a father who had a considerable monthly income of at least twenty thousand kuruş, he believed his own philosophical ideas to be more refined than any number of Platos—that is, he appreciated his own virtue and maturity, and accordingly decided that in this world, a man with a twenty thousand kuruş income didn't need anything else, so he always went on an outing on Fridays. Saturdays he rested from the previous day's exertions, and on Sundays couldn't *not* return to the pleasure spots, as going on outings on Sundays was considered even more *alafranga*. As for Sundays' weariness, he recuperated from that on Mondays. On Tuesdays, although he typically prepared to go to the office, whenever the weather was suitable his desire to visit places in Beyoğlu and see his father's old friends and companions got the better of him, so he would declare that day a holiday as well. If he made it into the office at all on Wednesdays, he only found enough time to talk about his exploits for three hours in the early afternoon and usually returned home with two hangers-on. As they were young like him and as Felâtun Bey lived in Beyoğlu, he had to amuse his friends *alafranga* style, so he spent those nights at *alafranga* places of entertainment. Since he burned the midnight oil those evenings, he slept much of the day Thursdays. Finally Friday would come around again and the next week repeated a similar pattern.

What can a young man possibly learn if he goes to the office only three hours per week and spends that time telling stories?

What do you mean, what can he learn? See, Felâtun Bey has learned a lot! He knows how to write, how to read. He knows French; he is intelligent, clever, and articulate. Most especially, his father has a monthly income of twenty thousand kuruş. What else is there to learn in this world?

Look, to be fair, let us say this: Felâtun Bey took an enormous interest in new publications. It was inconceivable for Felâtun Bey to admit, "I haven't heard of it," whenever someone said, "My dear, a new story has just been published." Every time a new book came out, the distributor was in the habit of taking Felâtun Bey's book right away to the Beyoğlu bookbinder H—— who, after binding it *alafranga* style and gilding the letters A and P on its back, would hand it to Felâtun Bey's servant to take home to him, so that when he came home at night, he would find the book and place it in his very neat library.

You know these two French letters, right? One of them is the letter A and the other, P. The former is the first letter of Felâtun Bey's first name, Ahmed, and the latter is the first letter of Plato, the French word for

Felâtun. In *alafranga*, there is a practice of inscribing the first letter or letters of one's name on a book and that's called one's "emblem."

Don't get us wrong, our purpose is not to criticize Felâtun Bey here; far from it, we intend to introduce his character to the reader. Therefore, let's add this piece of information as well:

Even though one would expect Felâtun Bey to be overwhelmingly arrogant given his wealth and self-assurance, his demeanor was quite otherwise. You know what it's like to be *alafranga*! He had to act modestly toward everyone and smile to everyone's face! In fact, sometimes when Felâtun Bey's servant saw his master speaking with someone very pleasantly, courteously, and respectfully, he would assume, "This gentleman must be a close friend of my master's." But the servant would be astonished and not know what to think after witnessing Felâtun erupt in rage and swear like a sailor upon parting from that person. Old-fashioned people would find it inappropriate and dishonorable to be courteous to someone face-to-face but then to curse them violently behind their back. *Alafrangas*, however, find this code of honor almost foolish.

We just mentioned Felâtun Bey's servant but haven't even touched upon his situation. This poor Mehmet, who had recently come from Kastamonu and who did not know much about the world, was enchanted by his stipend of a hundred kuruş per month, and was a man who expected a sympathetic slap on the back as praise. He managed to learn not only that his master had a son and a daughter but also that the son's name was "Pantolon Bey" (Master Pants) and the daughter's "Merdivan Hanım" (Miss Stairs).

What were you thinking! It certainly requires a fair amount of intelligence to be able to migrate from the name Felâtun to the word "Pantolon" (pants) and from the name Mihriban to the word "Merdivan" (stairs). Although poor Mehmet would call his real master "Merakli Efendi," he knew he was not saying it right and felt embarrassed since his master's name actually did not contain the letter L. Besides, back when Mehmet was in his hometown, he had even managed to read two dozen of the shorter Quranic verses!

Don't be surprised that Meraki Efendi, despite his *alafranga* lifestyle, employed a man like Mehmet at his mansion. The plan was to civilize him. In fact, he even started instructing him in manners. One day Meraki Efendi asked Mehmet, "What is your master doing?" and Mehmet replied, "He is eating his soup." Meraki Efendi corrected him, "Boy, don't say it that way, in *alafranga* they say 'he is eating *la soupe*.'" And when Mehmet said, "No, Sir, God forbid! He is not eating his 'suit,' he is eating soup!" Meraki Efendi understood Mehmet's confusion and counseled, "Son! In *alafranga* soup is called *la soupe*! You should learn this bit by bit." So, now you can see how Mehmet, too, was gradually becoming *alafranga*.

How could he not? Is there any other way? Regardless of how his father spoke, Felâtun Bey never uttered a word in anything but French! He said *"café au lait"* when he wanted coffee with milk, and Mehmet would willy-nilly memorize this by shuffling through different words he had learned earlier, like *kovala* (to chase) or *karyola* (bedstead).

In case you were wondering about Felâtun Bey's clothing, it is indescribable. Let us say this much, you know those latest fashion pictures in front of the clothing stores and tailor shops in Beyoğlu? Felâtun Bey would have a few hundred of them and he'd take the picture, get in front of a full-length mirror, and do everything possible to resemble the picture. For this reason, nobody ever saw him in the same clothes twice, so you could never hear anyone say, "That looks like Felâtun Bey's coat!"

We can, however, briefly describe his physique. He was a young man of roughly medium height, fragile-looking stature, yellowish complexion, black eyes and eyebrows. His hair, mouth, nose, and other features all depicted a beauty that would make a woman say, "He'll do." That's enough about Felâtun Bey for now, let us briefly turn to Mihriban Hanım.

It was clear from everything about her that she was Felâtun Bey's sister. Naturally, as one would expect of a girl, she was prettier.

Mihriban Hanım didn't know how to embroider the way other girls do. For *alafrangas* don't do that sort of thing. She didn't even know how to knit a pouch, socks, or anything, since *modistes* knit those. They are also the ones who do embroidery. There are many artificial flowers in Beyoğlu! Why would she bother to make them? It was the servants' job to do the laundry and ironing, and the cook's job to prepare the food. In fact, even brushing one's own hair is not an *alafranga* thing, so a coiffeur would come for the sole purpose of brushing her hair.

Although *alafranga* girls were expected to read, write, and have an education, poor Mihriban grew up without a mother, so couldn't manage to do this. For her musical education, her father hired a superb piano teacher. However, since this teacher played by herself while Mihriban's father listened, she didn't learn anything apart from the following tune: A snake lies underneath the stone/Whose eyebrows rise respectfully.

This song would make her lighthearted and cheerful! She would jump up and down and dance about with joy! Once she came of marriageable age, various people came to visit. Her father's fortune attracted all sorts of fortune hunters. When mothers of eligible sons came to investigate Mihriban Hanım, she'd ask them what their sons did for a living, and if they said "clerk," she'd say, "Ah! Penniless!" If they said "soldier," she'd picture their shoes and say "slipper wearer." If they said "cleric," she'd picture their turban and say "garlic head!" In this way, she would make up a pretext to reject them all. God forbid if the visitors said, "Oh! Young lady! Why are you saying this? Our son has this quality and that quality," she would laugh gaily and walk away saying, "Ay! Am I that desperate to marry your son? Go and look elsewhere!"

How about that? Are you surprised at Mihriban Hanım's independence? Don't be. Forasmuch as, having grown up as the mistress of the house, she'd appear in front of the visitors as both a potential bride as well as the mother of the bride. She would assume the role of her own mother when she rejected her visitors. Look, if you are going to be surprised, be surprised at this independent mother of the bride!

Are you weary of hearing about Felâtun Bey, Mustafa Meraki Efendi, and Mihriban Hanım? I ask for your forgiveness and with your permission, would like to say this final thing about them:

When the family was all together, Meraki Efendi and Felâtun Bey knew that if they criticized one of Mihriban Hanım's hair accessories or the way she wore her gloves, the poor girl would cry for three days and three nights. So even if she were to wear a flowerpot in her hair, they'd feel obliged to swear that it suited her very well. As for Meraki Efendi, even when he didn't agree with his son's ideas, he nevertheless felt compelled to pretend to agree with them, in order not to be embarrassed in front of a son who was, after all, named Felâtun and who never hesitated to point out his father's ignorance. What's more, poor Meraki Efendi would go so far as to claim that he had been thinking exactly the same thing for the last forty years. As a matter of fact, one day when they were discussing why days get longer and shorter, Mustafa Meraki Efendi abstained from stating his ideas on the subject and waited eagerly for his son to state his erudite opinion. Even when his son said, "Since the weather is cloudy in the winter the clouds postpone the arrival of sunlight," his father said, "Wonderful! Praise be! This renders even the Platos of the world impotent! Honestly, I am of the same opinion but just wanted to hear your thoughts on this."

Believe me when I say that this poor fellow accepted his son's ideas as pure wisdom. After some pleading and entreating, Meraki Efendi even had Felâtun write an essay on the subject, which he took to the printing house of one of the scientific magazines and returned enraged when it was rejected.

Chapter 2

THE PREVIOUS SECTION informed us pretty well about the specific personality of one of the two individuals we named our story after. Now, here briefly once again, we need to take a look at Râkım Efendi's situation.

Twenty-four years ago when the young man we call Râkım Efendi was one year old, he lost his father, one of the security guards of the vizier in Tophane, and was left in his mother's care. What can a security guard possibly bequeath to his child? Our Râkım Efendi's father handed down nothing that could be considered property except for a decrepit three-room henhouse near the famous Tuesday market of Salıpazarı, and an Arab slave.

His mother was a good woman, and her Arab female slave, Fedayi, was maybe even a better woman, so when his mother collected herself and recovered from the grief of her husband's death, she said, "Fedayi! Let's leave this lady and slave business aside. We have no choice but to work together to feed ourselves and this poor little boy." Yet Fedayi offered to take the entire burden on herself, replying, "Oh, my lady! Why should you work? I will work. I'll feed you, and my little master, my child." But Râkım Efendi's mother didn't leave all the work to Fedayi. She stitched and sewed embroidery, which she had Fedayi sell in the Salıpazarı market. On other days she sent Fedayi to grand houses to do laundry and clean, and sometimes even went herself. In short, they made their living through their own labors without relying on anyone else.

Râkım grew up. He was sent to the Taş Elementary School in Salıpazarı when he was five and transferred to the Valide Secondary School when he was eleven. At sixteen he left that school and managed to get accepted at the Ministry of Foreign Affairs.

9

My, how that young man worked! You know how they say, "He works day and night"? He actually did work day and night. Can you believe that his mother died just after he achieved this success?

But even this was a kind of blessing. She always used to say, "Oh! My dear Râkım! I would die satisfied if I could see you achieve some standing in this world," and she did attain this longed-for blessing.

At this point, Râkım still didn't earn a regular salary. Loyal Fedayi continued to sew, embroider napkins, stitch coffee bags, do laundry, and mop floors. She kept enough of her earnings to cover household expenses and gave the remainder to Râkım, thinking, "He is a young man and shouldn't want for money." Except that Râkım didn't need very much pocket money. What would a boy like him need money for anyway? Every morning he went to school in Süleymaniye, and in the afternoon went to the Ministry of Foreign Affairs, then took French lessons at the ministry, proceeded to practice his French at a doctor's office in Galata, arrived home in the evening, and after dinner went to Beyoğlu by way of the Kazancılar neighborhood to help his Armenian friend from the Ministry of Foreign Affairs read Turkish. In exchange for this service, he was permitted to browse through his Armenian friend's many French books.

It was said that even on Fridays Râkım spent the entire day in his Armenian friend's library. So it was that on Sundays, too, when the Ministry of Foreign Affairs was closed, Râkım would go to his friend's library. The members of the household developed such confidence in Râkım that they trusted him with their library, even when they were not at home. How pleasant those days were for Râkım!

Our Râkım Efendi pursued his education this way for four full years. His nanny, Fedayi, worked herself to the bone in the public kitchens to provide a proper upbringing for Râkım, the light of her mistress' life. Far from leaving this young man, who had been entrusted to her, in need, Fedayi managed to allow him to live in comfortable circumstances.

Even children from well-to-do families aren't vouchsafed the sort of education and training that Râkım Efendi received. Thanks to his own aspirations and his nanny's guidance and encouragement, in addition to Arabic grammar and syntax, he thoroughly learned the fourth annotated Arabic textbook. He was especially well trained in logic. He acquired a substantial knowledge of Hadith and Quranic exegesis. He even dipped into Islamic jurisprudence. Quite apart from finishing the Persian works of Saadi's *Gulistan* and *Bustan*, Jami's *Baharistan*, Attar's *Pandnameh*, and the poetry of Hafez and Saib, he memorized the most famous selections of these works. Now, about French: he achieved a good grasp of the language. Later, thanks to his good friend in Galata, he mastered the basics of physics, chemistry, and biology; in his Armenian friend's library in Beyoğlu he accumulated additional knowledge of geography, history, law, and international agreements. He never stopped reading French novels, plays, poems, and literature. Given the permission to take a book home for two nights, he wouldn't be content with only reading it, but would also copy out its best parts. This is how Râkım Efendi used to live. Narrow financial circumstances persisted until he was twenty. Even though the salary he was receiving from the ministry had reached 150 kuruş by that time, everyone knew that this was insufficient for a minister in the Foreign Affairs office.

One day a publisher friend of Râkım Efendi's brought him a French book. He offered to pay him approximately twenty gold coins if he agreed to translate the book into Turkish. Though the book numbered almost two hundred sizable pages, Râkım courageously agreed to translate it within a week. It ended up taking more like twelve days before Râkım delivered the translation to the press. The publisher promptly gave him twenty liras.

How about that? Who could estimate Râkım Efendi's happiness when he received this money!

No one. No one could estimate it. Poor Râkım had never seen that much money in any one place besides the moneylenders' coffers in Galata. Although he had long desired it, he couldn't even have imagined the possibility of making that much money from his own labors. Now when he saw this fortune, this treasure in his palm, he still couldn't believe that it belonged to him. Only after contemplating it for a while was he able to accept that it was indeed his, and he couldn't hold back his tears.

Does this surprise you? Look, honorable readers! If there's anyone among you who grew up like Râkım, think back on the first money you made through your own efforts, and how happy this made you feel. Remember that? Now it's out of place to ask, "What is so extraordinary about a man having twenty liras?" Well, it's not just any person. It is our very own Râkım Efendi, who always endeavored to be a decent man and had never seen twenty liras in one place before in his life.

After receiving the money, this poor young man ran straight back to his house and showed it to his loyal nanny. Guess what? When this good woman saw the money, she was appalled. "My Goodness! Sir, where did you find this? You didn't . . ." She came very close to translating her wicked thought into words but Râkım quickly explained how he made the money whereupon she was delighted. She said, "Oh! If only your mother was alive to see that you've earned these four pouches all at once! God bless her soul!" She couldn't keep herself from crying, and so Râkım also broke into tears once again.

Later they started thinking about how to spend their fortune. For even though we told you that Râkım had never had this much money, we never said he was greedy. On the contrary, since Râkım had grown up poor but contented, when he finally had this much money in his hands, he thought hording it was inappropriate. Instead, money was a means to happiness. He enjoyed earning money to spend it on their well-being. And when his nanny declared, "Sir! I think we could spend this money on a new set of clothes for you," Râkım said, "No, my dear Nanny! What I have is enough. Our first priority is to save you from serving others. For you are getting older." So they put half of the money aside and agreed to spend 150 kuruş every two weeks to supplement their expenditures over the next four months. They used the other half to repair their house, which had started to fall into ruins.

Anyone who knows anything at all knows that the first sale of the day, just as with every new beginning, comes with a blessing. And that's exactly what happened with Râkım. Using what he had learned from studying the foreign newspapers that were always available at the Porte, he developed a broad understanding of diplomacy and occasionally wrote articles for some newspapers. Although he submitted these with no expectation of payment, the publisher started pressing one or two liras into his hands every week or so to encourage him. In fact, later on these payments grew more substantial. So much so that when it came to the point when he was making two liras a week, he decided to quit his job at the Ministry of Foreign Affairs.

We were saddened by his departure from the ministry because if he had stayed there, there was no doubt that he would have excelled.

Meanwhile, Râkım added to the number of his European friends. This provided him with more opportunities for translation and petition-writing in European languages. The foreigners who needed to write things like Turkish memorandums, documents, protests, or petitions would hand the work over to Râkım.

Why become verbose? After pursuing this path for a couple years, he was making as much as twenty or thirty liras a month. However, in order to earn this money, the poor young man had to work seventeen hours a day, and only spent seven hours sleeping, resting, eating, and drinking.

He renovated his house in Salıpazarı and furnished it nicely according to his own tastes. He began to accumulate books for a library by collecting the most distinguished books in Turkish and French. Despite all these expenditures, Râkım still had plenty of money left over.

His nanny tried to get Râkım married several times. Râkım always said he had no need to marry. Loyal Fedayi didn't want Râkım to take a bride only for his sake; she also needed a helpmate in her old age. Râkım recognized that she needed help and decided to purchase a female slave for the household.

His nanny ordered some Arab female slaves from a couple of slave traders to come to the house for inspection. Fedayi tried them out for a day or two but found that she always disliked them and ended up returning them. One day Râkım Efendi took a shortcut through Karabaş to go from Tophane up to Beyoğlu to get to Kumbaracı Yokuşu Street. On his way, he saw a lovely Circassian girl and an elderly, white-bearded Circassian man knocking on a door. When he looked more carefully at the girl, something about her spoke to him. As he continued on his way, he thought to himself, "Why bother? My nanny doesn't want a white slave, she wants an Arab; this girl won't do."

Râkım began walking away but found himself rooted to the spot! Why, you ask? Even Râkım himself didn't know why. Saying, "What if I simply inquire about this girl? No one can force me to buy her anyway!" he turned back and knocked on the door that had now closed behind the Circassian girl and the elderly man.

Somebody opened the door. Râkım asked for the elderly man; he came. Râkım inquired whether the girl was a slave and if so, whether she was for sale. She *was* for sale. He wanted to see her. They showed him. She was a tall, dark-eyed girl with a little mouth, a fine nose, and a pleasant body, yet because she was very thin, diseased, and only fourteen, she wasn't something that would appeal to everyone. But those languid looks! That melancholy smile!

How did Râkım come to be holding her hand? Probably because he had taken it in astonishment and it hadn't crossed his mind to let it go. He asked the elderly man for her price. Did he say, "one hundred gold coins?"

The man mentioned her price. And what did Râkım do? He cried like a child. And what did the girl do? She started crying, too!

The elderly man didn't know what to make of it. He asked Râkım if she reminded him of someone he knew but received no reply.

No, she didn't resemble anyone he knew.

Here is some news: Râkım was crying tears of joy and thanking God for giving an orphan like him the opportunity to buy such a beautiful white slave. Indeed! This was the kind of sensitive and emotional young man Râkım was. He said to the elderly man, "I'm not asking whether this girl has a price or not. We are talking about her freedom here. I admit that freedom is priceless. However, I don't have more than eighty liras. If you agree to this amount, I'll take her." Seeing Râkım cry, the elderly man regretted not asking for 150 gold coins, and when he said that he couldn't reduce the price, Râkım replied, "In that case, if you give me a month to collect twenty gold coins, I'll take her." They agreed on it and the elderly man handed the slave girl over to Râkım immediately since he wanted to dispose of the girl as soon as possible, suspecting that she might have tuberculosis.

What do you think? Remember that we told you how Râkım was holding the girl's hand? Well, now that she was his property, he let it go!

Râkım abandoned his trip to Beyoğlu and went back home to Salıpazarı, accompanied by the elderly man. He took the girl into his house and asked his nanny to go get the money. He counted out eighty gold coins and handed them over to the slave trader. Râkım then collected four or five people that he knew from Tophane to witness his signing a promissory note for the remaining twenty gold coins, before sending the slave trader on his way.

While walking back home after this transaction, he was plagued by regret and anxiety. "I wonder what my nanny will say about this. I acted just like a child! I should have asked for my nanny's opinion. She is like a mother to me, after all." When he came home, his nanny welcomed him saying, "Oh, Sir! You got a great deal! What a warmhearted girl! Did you buy her for me as a helpmate? Well, let's name her Janan then." Poor Râkım was so glad that he had pleased his nanny and agreed to the name.

You should know that Râkım wasn't the type of man to neglect his job just because he bought a female slave. On that same day, he had two important jobs in Beyoğlu, so he got up and went off to Beyoğlu by way of Kazancılar. One of the two jobs was to see the Armenian Mr. G——. In fact, just the night before, Mr. G—— sent his manservant to tell Râkım that he expected to see him no matter what. His house was in Ağahamamı. Râkım got there and found Mr. G—— home. Mr. G—— wanted Râkım to compose a letter to the governor of Silistra, which would then be delivered along with the sheep taxes by one of his men.

In just fifteen minutes, Râkım drafted and made a fair copy of this letter, had Mr. G—— seal it, sealed it again himself and left it on a cabinet next to Mr. G——. While Râkım was waiting to see if there were any other requests, Mr. G—— called for his pay clerk and had him settle accounts with Râkım. Mortified that his continued presence might have been misunderstood as a request for payment, Râkım explained, "I was only waiting to see if you have any other orders." Mr. G——, being an Ottoman gentleman, joked, "Isn't what I ordered also an order? I would like to see this order carried out as well." A short while later, the pay clerk entered with an account of all the documents Râkım had written for him in the last three months.

Mr. G—— picked up the account and began reading:

"For writing the letter to the governor of Bursa, requesting permission to collect the remaining sheep taxes from the Bursa province . . . ten liras . . . For writing the response to the response . . . ten liras . . . For writing that impressive six-page document to the Ministry of Finance concerning the yearly examination of the attached written accounting of the Varna district tithe and sheep taxes . . . and pieces of related letters . . . eight liras."

After going through this list, Mr. G—— smoothly proposed, "I won't pay for any of this. But I have to concede that the Bursa taxes, which I had completely given up on, were only paid due to the eloquence of your letter. And for that reason, I'll pay you something." Having said that, he ordered his pay clerk to give Râkım thirty liras.

Oh! What joy! Oh, what gratitude! He was so grateful that tears welled up in his eyes. But grateful for what exactly? Well, of God's generosity for offering such opportunities to an orphan like himself!

After receiving his payment, he went onto his second job. This second job involved a fairly aristocratic English family that had just arrived from England and settled into a house on Asmalımescit Street. Râkım didn't know what the job was; he went there because one of his friends told him there was a job to be had. When he arrived, his friend was already there. Apparently the job entailed tutoring the English family's two daughters in Turkish once a week.

How could Râkım possibly reject a job like this? A workhorse like him! He happily accepted it. He didn't bother inquiring about the salary but his friend suggested that the family pay him one British lira per lesson. Râkım blushed with modesty and gratitude for God's grace. After accepting the job, he strolled down the Kumbaracı Yokuşu Street without feeling his feet touch the ground. He arrived at Karabaş in the Tophane neighborhood, and when he came across the elderly Circassian man in the Slave Traders' Coffeehouse, he said, "Come here my dear Sir, come here, I don't like to have debts. I collected the money. Thank God a thousand times for sending the money from such an unexpected place!" He paid the twenty-gold-coin debt off and freed himself of it. Although unnecessary, he even contacted the witnesses of the promissory note to let them know it had been paid off. He then put the remaining fortune of ten gold coins into his pocket and headed home.

How happy his loyal nanny was after Râkım delivered the good news! Fedayi's fondness for the girl multiplied! In addition to the name Janan, she gave her the nickname "Blessed."

Now we've told you about the second person whose name adorns our story.

Chapter 3

RÂKIM AND HIS NANNY started educating and refining Janan, whom they considered to be God's blessing and generous gift. The poor girl really was ill. On the second day after Janan's arrival, Râkım went to see a physician friend in order to ensure personalized attention, rather than simply summoning a doctor. He described Janan's desperate medical condition. They got on a coach together and came back to the house. After examining the girl in great detail and asking her about her symptoms, the physician assured them: "There's nothing to worry about. She probably contracted the illness in the Caucasus. Now that she has moved from the Caucasus to Istanbul's warm climate, she will recover on her own. I will prescribe a medicine for her. You should boil around five hundred grams of pure cow's milk and have her drink it very hot every morning after she wakes up. She shouldn't wander around dusty places or injure her chest by singing. Make sure that she breathes fresh air from time to time, so take her to wide-open areas and to the sea. You shouldn't tire her out to the point where she has to gasp for breath. God willing, she will be just fine. It's really nothing anyway! I'm suggesting that you take these measures merely as a precaution. She is a beautiful girl, may God protect her."

Although his nanny didn't understand the type of illness these arrangements addressed, Râkım did. He saw the doctor on his way with gratitude and told his nanny to carry out the aforementioned procedures meticulously. Do you think poor Fedayi needed any urging to provide care for such a poor girl? Initially Janan had entered the house to ease Fedayi's workload but now the tables had turned and Fedayi was willing

18

to give up her own comfort to assist the girl. When Arabs are good, they are really good.

While Janan is receiving her treatment and education, let us turn to another part of our story:

Râkım had agreed to devote Fridays to tutoring the two daughters of the English family in Asmalımescit. So, on the first Friday, he left his house to go there early in the afternoon.

Since one of the main characters in our story is from this family, we need to provide some more information about them. We mentioned earlier that this English family was aristocratic. Indeed, they were. They were aristocrats, but not members of the nobility like barons or dukes. After accumulating five hundred thousand British liras in a paper trading business, the Englishman quit commercial life and came to Istanbul to spend the rest of his life in comfort. In fact, since he didn't have any sons and his family comprised a wife and two daughters, he calculated that given his fortune, many men would want to marry his girls and thought his wife would also live happily in this way. Now no business, no idea, no thought could prevent this Englishman from pursuing a life of comfort.

The name he inherited from his ancestors was Ziklas, and naturally his wife was referred to as Mrs. Ziklas. Although his girls could also be called Miss Ziklas, within the household the elder one was called Jan, and the younger one, Margaret. This family hailed from Canterbury. The town's proximity to France, together with their trade business, led them to develop social relations with the French. That's why every member of the family could speak French very well. Râkım was confident that he'd be able to teach the girls successfully; after all, he too was fluent in French.

You know how they say, "two sides of the same coin?" Well, Jan and Margaret were a perfect example of this. Both were tall and delicate like saplings but also had really rosy cheeks, deep blue eyes, and whitish flaxen hair. That's just how English girls are!

One might assume from our description that looking at their faces wouldn't set one's heart aflutter. Don't rush to judgment. Every girl has her own unique beauty and, as we well know, can skillfully employ it to pierce the hearts of her admirers.

Râkım wrote the letters of the Turkish alphabet "ا (aleph) ب (be) پ (pe) ت (te) ث (se) ج (jim) چ (chim) ح (he) خ (khe) د (dal) ذ (zal) ر (re) ز (ze) ژ (zhe)," et cetera, with a thick pen on a piece of good quality English paper, and taught them to spell their names. He asked them to memorize these letters in a week and took his leave.

Oh, esteemed writer! Is that really all that happened? Didn't they talk about anything? Not even with their father or mother?

No! That was it for that day. Concerned about his nanny and Janan, he made his way rapidly by way of Kumbaracı Yokuşu Street down to Tophane, and as he had enough money, took a coach to his house in Salıpazarı.

Well, well! Doesn't he travel by foot anymore?

No, no, you misunderstand! Let me explain: The family gave him an extra lira to permit him to come and go by coach. Since God, in His graciousness, bestowed this extra income specifically for this purpose, Râkım Efendi felt obliged to travel to and from Beyoğlu by coach in appreciation of this blessing. It even troubled him not to ride on a coach in the morning. You see, this was the kind of contract Râkım had with God. It was quite remarkable.

His nanny usually welcomed him when he returned home, but on that night Janan greeted him at the door. Râkım sensed Janan's demeanor changing every day. Thanks to his nanny's care and devotion, Janan was always neat, and her color was improving. Nevertheless, Râkım couldn't understand why his nanny hadn't greeted him at the front door, and felt compelled to ask:

RÂKIM: My dear Nanny, I am used to seeing your face every night when I come home. I see that this custom changed tonight.

FEDAYI: My dear son, my master! What is the point in seeing my black face as soon as you come home, now that God has given us a beautiful white female slave?

RÂKIM (*throwing his arms around her and kissing her affectionately*): No, my dear Nanny, no! Your face is as sweet as a mother's face to me. If a *houri* came down from heaven, she would not be more beautiful than you are to me. I want to see your blessed face every night. If not, I swear you'll force me to banish

Janan from here. Besides, don't make her do this. She is just a child. She might get ideas. As for myself, I don't have any such intentions.

FEDAYI: Ah, my dear Sir, but why not?

RÂKIM: I told you already! If you love me like your child, then you will honor my wishes.

After having this talk with his nanny, Râkım called Janan over and showed her the Turkish alphabet, thinking, "I started teaching the English girls today! Let's see how this Circassian girl does. Will she learn faster than them?" Just imagine the joy she felt! Indeed, since the Circassian was very eager to learn to read, there couldn't be a better way to display his fondness for her.

It became clear from the first week that Janan was going to do better than the English girls. After all, Râkım spent every evening teaching Janan and although she learned quickly, she often urged him to repeat the lessons.

At the same time, Râkım had been teaching the English girls for a month now and managed to teach them not only the alphabet but also the different forms of the letters and how to use them in a word. That is, which shapes the Turkish letters take when they appear at the beginning, in the middle, or at the end of a word. He also taught them the vowel markers, and started having them write words like *papa, pen, desk*, and *ear*. However, they didn't compare to Janan. In addition to being able to write four- and five-syllable words within a month, she was able to combine them with the pronouns, *My, your, his, her, its, our, your, their.*

This shows that Râkım was progressing along the path he had chosen for himself as a teacher. Yes, that's right, indeed he was.

Who do you suppose Râkım ran across one Friday as he was on his way to Mr. Ziklas's house as usual? What if I said Felâtun Bey! Yes, that's exactly right. Upon entering the house, Râkım found Felâtun Bey quizzing the girls in his own fashion. When Felâtun Bey saw Râkım Efendi, he smiled and spoke in French, so that the English could understand:

FELÂTUN (*surprised*): Look who's here! So it is you who is teaching these ladies?

RÂKIM (*uneasily*): Yes Sir, it's me!

MR. ZIKLAS: Oh! So this means that you know one another?

FELÂTUN (*calmly*): Yes! I am very fond of this fellow, and I assume our feelings are mutual.

RÂKIM: Is there any man in this world that I don't like? I try my best to be on good terms with everyone, and I like everyone.

FELÂTUN (*to Râkım*): I met Mr. and Mrs. Ziklas two months ago. You have been coming to this house for over a month now but somehow we haven't run into each other.

RÂKIM: It was destined to be today then, Sir.

FELÂTUN: It was my father who introduced me to the family. He had the honor of knowing them before I did. Later, he brought me along and introduced me to Mr. and Mrs. Ziklas and their daughters.

MRS. ZIKLAS: Indeed! We don't know how to thank his excellency your father for his kindness.

FELÂTUN (*adding humility to his calm demeanor*): Not at all, Sir. It's your kindness.

After some casual conversation, Râkım said,

RÂKIM: Dear Sir, would you excuse us? Shall we get started with the lesson?

FELÂTUN (*with that blessed smile still on his face*): By all means! In fact, I was quizzing the ladies just now.

RÂKIM: Well, did you find their Turkish improving?

FELÂTUN (*still with that blessed smile*): Who am I to comment on the intelligence and comprehension of these ladies? Yet, my friend, I see certain things in these lessons that I can't quite make sense of. Do we have these "پ (pe), چ (che) and ژ (zhe)" letters in the alphabet? When we were in school, we learned the alphabet as, "ا (aleph) ب (be) ت (te) ث (se) ج (jim) ح (chem) ح (he) خ (khe) د (dal) ذ (zal) ر (re) ز (ze)." I don't seem to remember those three letters? What are they?

JAN: Yes, dear teacher! This is what Felâtun Bey said. We're confused.

RÂKIM: No, no, far from it! There's nothing to be confused about here. Felâtun Bey knows this perfectly well but must have forgotten. You're right, this is how we learned the alphabet in school. However, the alphabet we learned is only for Arabic. Turkish requires three more letters. Otherwise how would we write *pasha*, *chavoosh*, or *mozhdeh*? Surely we need those letters?

It seems that when Felâtun Bey initially saw these letters and didn't recognize them, he tried to appear like Plato in front of the English family. He insinuated that the tutor the family had hired didn't really know Turkish properly and that if the family employed such people, the girls wouldn't learn anything. He underestimated and mocked the tutor even though he didn't know who he was. When he heard Râkım's explanation, he blushed deeply:

FELÂTUN: Oh, yes! You're right. I got it.

MR. ZIKLAS: I agree with Râkım Efendi. We have a little book to help us with Turkish, and it also has those letters.

FELÂTUN: I remember them now, too, Sir. I have another question but would like to request the esteemed instructor's permission to ask it.

RÂKIM: Not at all, Sir! We are just trying to help these ladies. How wonderful if we could get some of your valuable suggestions.

FELÂTUN: Of course, Sir! Although we know the letter "ب (be)," we have not seen so many different forms of it! What I mean to say is, Sir, it would be better if these ladies' minds were not confused with such useless jumble.

MARGARET: But if we didn't learn these other forms, how could we possibly connect them to each other? The little Turkish instruction booklet my father mentioned is right here. Our instructor's lessons are consistent with the book and even better!

Margaret reached for the booklet to point out the forms of the letters in question but Râkım preempted her by taking up a pen and explaining, "Sir! Let's say we're writing a name, like *Mustafa*, in cursive. We don't write each letter separately. We connect them. Remember that letters take different forms depending on whether they come at the beginning, in the middle or at the end of a word." As soon as he pointed this out, Felâtun Bey realized his mistake and his embarrassment intensified.

Come on now! How is it possible that Felâtun didn't know the alphabet?

Well, it wasn't that he didn't know but there are some men who don't know how they learned the things they know. Especially in our country, most people who know don't know how they learned. Felâtun Bey was one of those people. He didn't know how he learned what he knew. Why does this surprise you? We even knew a clerk with beautiful handwriting who connected every letter when composing formal ministry documents. And yet he wasn't able to explain the rules of his own handwriting!

Due to his intense embarrassment, Felâtun Bey didn't want to stay any longer and soon made his departure. After he left, Râkım didn't utter a word concerning what Felâtun Bey knew or didn't know and got on with doing his job. In the afternoon, when he was about to take his leave, he said to the family, "Really, meeting once a week isn't enough for these ladies and besides I consider your payment to be too much in return for my service. With your permission, I'd like to come and tutor them twice a week." They quickly accepted his request.

Do you wonder how close Râkım Efendi became with the Ziklas household in the matter of a month? So close that the family no longer saw him as only a teacher. They respected him so much that they considered him a family friend and an honorable, well-mannered, modest, wise, and mature individual.

That night, Râkım returned home a bit early and encountered something extraordinary at the house. Janan wasn't there.

RÂKIM: Nanny! Where is Janan?

FEDAYI: She is here, Sir.

RÂKIM: Here, where? Our house is made up of three rooms and an anteroom. I looked everywhere but she is nowhere to be found!

FEDAYI (*sharply*): She's here, Sir. She should be back soon.

RÂKIM: Now come on, wherever she is, tell me. If she is somewhere unmentionable, still tell me. Do you want me to think that you are engaging in some secret business?

FEDAYI: To tell the truth, we decided to do something without your knowledge, but I fear that we've made a mistake.

RÂKIM (*anxiously*): What's going on, my dear?

FEDAYI: Nothing. Our neighbor, —— Bey hired a piano teacher to provide piano lessons for his female slaves. We felt eager to do the same. We feared that if we told you, you might not have allowed it.

RÂKIM (*a bit angry*): True, my dear Nanny! Of course I wouldn't! And I still don't! If Janan wants to learn to play the piano, God, who hasn't turned down any of our wishes, would also make this happen. Should I tell you what I really think? I don't consent to Janan leaving the house without you accompanying her. As long as you are with her, take her wherever you want. This is a strange world. And it would be a shame if we squandered the good manners we've taught her.

Poor Râkım uttered these words so earnestly that Fedayi couldn't help but understand his point. Janan returned home half an hour later. When she found her master home, she approached him shaking fearfully. Râkım realized that if he were to say something harsh, she might faint. Accordingly,

RÂKIM: Come here, Janan. Come, don't be scared my dear. Now, I warned my nanny. From now on whenever you want to go somewhere, you are allowed to go with her. However, I don't give you permission to leave without her. Are you eager to play the piano, sweetheart? I will buy you a piano and hire a female teacher for you as well.

The poor little girl was expecting her master to scold her but was offered a piano instead. She felt like hugging her master out of happiness and wanted to thank him. Yet, she couldn't manage to find the right words in Turkish.

After this conversation, the desire to obtain a piano and find a piano teacher was at the forefront of Râkım's mind. Every evening, whenever he looked at her face, he'd think that she was asking, "What about your promise?" At the time, his income, which was about twenty-five or thirty liras, wasn't enough to pay for a piano, but he could easily borrow some money. The real difficulty would be paying for an instructor who would cost four or five liras a month.

One day Râkım was at one of his French friends, Mathieu Ancel's house, in Beyoğlu. A few ladies were playing the piano in the living room, including Mathieu's wife and sister. Like everyone else, this family liked Râkım and took pleasure in his company. In fact, upon Râkım's indirect request, a beautiful brunette lady situated herself in front of the piano and played some traditional *alaturka* songs like "The falling tress of hair," and "In your beauty." Those present thought these songs would please Râkım, and so were puzzled to see him sorrowful. They even inquired why he looked so sad. Although Râkım tried to brush it off by saying, "You know how silly I get sometimes," some thought that Râkım was burning with love, and others interpreted it differently. So Râkım had to explain, "No, no ladies and gentlemen! My heart is very sensitive. Yet it's not chained to anyone; it's completely free. It's something else. I have a slave who wishes to learn to play the piano. I heard that she was taking some piano lessons from a lady along with other female slaves. But she is very inexperienced and doesn't know much about the outside world, so I didn't let her continue for I was concerned about letting such a girl go there by herself. I promised to buy a piano for her, and now I am reminded of that . . ." As he was saying this, the brunette lady in front of the piano rose from her seat, "Yes, dear Sir! You took my most talented student from me. I can't teach anything to the other hussies! It's been five weeks since you prohibited her from taking lessons. She would have improved a lot more by now." Râkım was surprised at the coincidence:

RÂKIM: Oh, so you were her teacher, Madame?

BRUNETTE LADY: Yes, Sir, I had that honor.

RÂKIM: Don't mention it! But . . .

BRUNETTE LADY: You're excused if you prohibited her in order to protect her morals, for her fellow students are very naughty indeed.

MATHIEU: All right, but what we do now?

RÂKIM: To be honest Sir, the solution is to ask this lady to teach my girl, but . . .

MATHIEU: Yes, and that's the problem. Râkım can't afford a teacher who costs one lira.

BRUNETTE LADY: I wouldn't go to Râkım Efendi's house for a mere lira! I would go for something more substantial.

EVERYBODY: And what would that be?

BRUNETTE LADY: Something really big, Sir, huge! Râkım Efendi's friendship! If he pays me with his friendship, I can go to instruct his slave every week after I leave —— Bey's house.

RÂKIM (*gratefully*): We'd be honored.

BRUNETTE LADY: This is my offer! Take it or leave it.

This brunette lady's name was Josephine. Madame Josephine's promise made not only Râkım, but also everyone assembled there, happy.

JOSEPHINE: But look, there is one condition. I want an excellent piano. I won't have my fingers touch any old average piano. You should be prepared to sacrifice at least eight hundred francs to buy a good one.

EVERYBODY: Of course!

RÂKIM: I wouldn't want your fingers to touch any average piano either. However, I don't know how to choose a quality piano. Tell me which one you like, and I'll go and get it immediately.

JOSEPHINE: We'll go and choose one together.

Râkım was grateful for Josephine's kindness. Although Josephine explained that she was doing this more for Janan's sake than Râkım's, we know the real story. The female slaves at —— Bey's house couldn't learn anything because they were so frivolous. Janan, on the other hand, picked things up quickly. Josephine could use this to her advantage in the future. If —— Bey brought a suit against her for not being able to teach, she could say, "I gave this poor girl the same lessons. She learned very well but these girls didn't because they didn't practice." That's really why she agreed to help Râkım. But we digress. The point is that Râkım needed a lady instructor and found a really good one. What's more, she was willing to teach for free.

After leaving Mathieu's house, they went into a store in Kulekapı that sold musical instruments. There, Josephine picked out an excellent piano and Râkım bought it for seven hundred francs. Râkım paid four hundred in cash, and, upon Josephine's recommendation, requested a one-month extension for the rest. He had a porter carry the piano to his house.

Imagine Janan's delight! She almost went out of her mind! In the other room, she hugged and kissed her nanny! Râkım was touched by this scene. My, what an emotional man, this Râkım! His eyes filled with tears upon seeing Janan so happy. He sincerely expressed his gratitude towards the merciful God for granting her such pleasure.

Their house had three bedrooms, which they divided amongst themselves, and they furnished the living room to create some space for hosting guests. Since we've started talking about their house, come, let's cast glance at the inside:

The little house had only two stories. On the ground floor there was a kitchen, a pantry, and a woodshed; climbing upstairs one would reach a foyer and face a glass door that led onto the living room. To the right of the living room, facing the street, were two bedrooms, and across from the glass door was the third bedroom, and to its left, a bathroom. In the past, all of the rooms opened directly onto the living room, but with the renovations, Râkım had a wall of wood slats and plaster built to a create an L-shaped, one-meter-wide corridor to separate the bedrooms from the living room. This way all the rooms opened onto the corridor, which then connected onto the living room from a door on the right. The left side of the living room had three windows, and the one in the middle was sort of like what we call a French window, which resembled a glass door and faced the door giving onto the corridor on the right side of the living room. These windows opened to an approximately 230 square meter little garden, which was higher than the street, and one could easily go from the French window three steps down into this garden.

Now you understand the shape and division of the house! Paint the inside nicely, cover the walls with paper, put some nice rugs on the floor, place a small couch in the living room, add a mirror and a sideboard, and hang a fine painting on either side of the mirror. There, now you've formed an image of Râkım's living room in your mind. How nice this little living room will look with a piano across from the stairway entrance!

Râkım's room was the first of the two rooms on the right side. As you enter his room, you face the windows. On the right was his library. On the left was the bed. On both sides, there was also a cupboard containing antiques and odds and ends.

The room next to his was allocated to Janan. Actually, Râkım hadn't wanted to be her next-door neighbor but his nanny preferred the third room with a built-in wardrobe, so it became Janan's. As you enter the room, you see a bedstead on the left, and on the right a small dresser with a nice mirror and two vases, and a dresser set near the door. In front of the windows was a little table with some sewing accessories.

Let us also remind you that Râkım carried out his morning preparations in Janan's room because the only washbasin in the house was located there.

Now, about his nanny's room, which was located on the other side of the corridor, across from the stairway. Fedayi's room had no windows and was poorly lit from a window down the corridor facing the garden. It resembled those old-fashioned rooms with built-in wardrobes, and since the nanny didn't sleep on a bedstead, she would keep her *alaturka* bedding set in the built-in wardrobe. This room was also used as a general storage space. Both Râkım and Janan's clothing chests were stored in the lower sections of the built-in wardrobes.

Josephine arranged her lessons to take place on Thursdays. Râkım Efendi was home when she arrived the first Thursday afternoon. As soon as Janan saw her teacher at the door, she hugged her and expressed her pleasure in half-Circassian, half-Turkish. Josephine didn't understand a word of Turkish, so she hugged Janan back and told Râkım, "Monsieur Râkım! I don't understand this girl's language! But her eyes, stance and attitude all tell me what she's trying to say." Râkım felt content and grateful for Josephine's fondness toward Janan, and urged Josephine to consider this poor little girl more of a sister than a student.

Josephine found Râkım's living room pleasing. She particularly enjoyed looking at the trim and flourishing little garden from the living room window:

JOSEPHINE: Monsieur Râkım! I really like your house. You have such good taste! Honestly, your living room is cute and cozy. I'd like to see the other rooms as well.

RÂKIM: Madame, the rest of the house is just bedrooms.

JOSEPHINE: Don't be such a child! Aren't we going to be friends? Bedrooms or not, I still want to see them. You unmarried men all think this way, don't you!

Following this conversation, Râkım showed Madame Josephine the bedrooms. We don't have to explain Janan's natural talents at length, do we? Josephine found the rooms spotlessly clean. Everything was very orderly and in its place. She was so delighted that she repeatedly exclaimed: "How blissful to possess such a house and such a slave." Râkım introduced her to Fedayi, who, he explained, was like a second mother to him. Josephine overwhelmed her with compliments.

It had been three months since Janan first came to Râkım Efendi's house and one month since Josephine has last seen Janan. During this time,

Janan's education and care continued; her face took on new color and liveliness, and she grew increasingly beautiful. After finishing the lesson with Janan in half an hour, Josephine felt it necessary to have the following conversation with Râkım:

JOSEPHINE: Come on now, Monsieur Râkım! Your slave is very pretty, very smart, and very perceptive!

RÂKIM: Give her some time and she will open up even more, Madame.

JOSEPHINE: That's not what I am trying to say. You are young, and so is she! Two young people in one place! Not bad, eh?

RÂKIM: No, there you have the wrong idea.

JOSEPHINE: Why? As if it's something inappropriate?

RÂKIM: How could there be anything inappropriate? She's my private slave.

JOSEPHINE: Meaning what?

RÂKIM: But . . . I'll be much happier if I consider her like a sister.

JOSEPHINE: Wait a minute. Is she supposed to like you as a brother?

RÂKIM: If I treat her only with brotherly affection, how else could she feel? Surely she'll like me as a brother.

JOSEPHINE: You're just saying that for now, my dear. Let's wait and see, let's give it some time. Do you really think you are an angel? Have you sworn not to make the most of having a beautiful girl?

RÂKIM: No! I'd give a lot for such an opportunity but I wouldn't want to have that relationship with Janan.

JOSEPHINE: Oh well, whatever. Congratulations. That's all I'll say.

As Josephine said these last words, the clock indicated late afternoon, so she said goodbye to Râkım, Janan, and Fedayi, and took her leave.

Do you still remember why Janan was purchased in the first place? She was supposedly bought to help Fedayi, right? Poor Fedayi still found herself confined to the kitchen. Janan's assistance was limited to cleaning the house and doing the laundry once a week. She spent the rest of her time studying and sewing. Especially after starting the piano lessons, she didn't have any free time. When she was bored with studying, she would play the piano; when she was bored with the piano, she would start sewing, and loyal Fedayi was always gratified whenever she saw the little girl amusing herself.

Are you surprised that Fedayi didn't feel jealous of this girl? You shouldn't be! For she'd certainly put Janan in Râkım's arms if she had the chance. She'd sigh thinking, "Isn't my master an angel? He has a fairy in front of him and the idea of taking her doesn't even cross his mind." Whenever Fedayi came across a beautiful fabric, she would get Râkım to purchase it by saying, "Janan is young, she should dress up and look neat in your presence." She would then take it right away to a seamstress, implore her to cut it according to the latest fashion, whereupon she'd give it to Janan to sew into a dress for herself. After a while Janan didn't need anyone to cut the cloth for her! She would take a dress that fit her well, unstitch it to use as a template for the uncut cloth, and then sew and resew both dresses. The poor girl was already beautiful and enjoyed a fine figure, so whatever she wore fit her like a glove.

If there are any readers who think that Râkım doesn't deserve so many good things, we would like to remind them that they are being unfair. What merit would there be in education and knowledge if a man doesn't at least attain these rewards after performing eye-straining work day and night for seven or eight years and endeavoring to refine himself?

In terms of their education, the English girls were progressing as quickly as Janan. The girls would ask their teacher for forty to fifty new words every week, record them in their notebooks, and memorize them; they even started speaking Turkish bit by bit. Their reading and writing skills showed particular improvement; they learned more in this short period than others could have in an entire year.

Due to the fondness and friendship this family showed him, Râkım started staying at their household for dinner. One Sunday, they were pleased to have Râkım accompany them to Kağıthane. In fact, there's more to come regarding their intimacy and friendship. Just like Râkım, Mister Ziklas also had a passion for the sea. He bought a nice, long skiff and entrusted it to Râkım's care in the Salıpazarı port. On certain Sundays Râkım would bring the boat to the harbor at Tophane, meet the English family there, and set sail for Kadıköy and the Princes' Islands. However, this boat cruise deserves further description, so let us indulge in a couple more lines.

It was customary for Jan and Margaret to put on their sailor outfits whenever they went on a boat ride. As part of their outfits, they had sailors' caps encircled by blue ribbons and another blue ribbon that tied under their chins. Their hair was brushed tightly into ponytails and fell over onto their shoulders. They also sported white, European shirts with blue sleeves and blue collars that had a little white anchor on them. On top of the shirts were sleeveless, short raincoats that they used only as necessary. They wore knee-length white skirts with suspenders made from the same blue ribbon, white socks that reached up to their thighs, and blue boots on their feet. They tied blue woolen sashes around their waists. And finally blue taffeta neckerchiefs completed their costumes.

When these two sailors sat on the rowing benches, Mr. Ziklas took the helm and Râkım sat across from Mrs. Ziklas. The two young girls furled and unfurled the sails. They always enjoyed a variety of snacks and the finest English beer. Râkım never tired of these pleasurable outings. In bad weather, when it became necessary to row, Mrs. Ziklas would take the helm, Margaret would sit on the forward bench, Râkım on the second, the older sister on the third, and their father on the backbench. As you know, while rowing, the English bend and pull their full weight on the oars until they are leaning back and a little to the side of the person sitting behind them. Râkım found himself resting against the elder sister, and the younger sister resting against him. This gave Râkım more delight than anything else. Yet, do you suppose he gave their parents any cause for concern?

Well! So . . . Râkım had such urges too, eh!

Why shouldn't he? Did we introduce Râkım to you as someone who doesn't understand appetites, masculinity, and femininity? Besides, the pleasure he felt was totally emotional and conscientious, and since he never thought of turning these desires into reality, he engendered no mistrust.

Talking about a boat trip, we just remembered the one Felâtun Bey took with the Ziklas family. It was a particularly windy day and they faced some sizeable waves off the coast of the Princes' Islands. As they started rocking up and down, the English took pleasure from watching the sea raise the boat and knock it down like a watermelon, whereas Felâtun Bey began shaking in his shoes and shouting, "Mummy! Mummy!" every time they rocked up and down. The English didn't understand anything he said but understood how scared and terrified he must have been from his appearance and have laughed about it a few times since then. They even told Râkım about it.

Have we started talking about Felâtun Bey again?

If so, there are a few other things we'd like to tell you about, so let's get to them.

Chapter 4

AS WINTER APPROACHED and the days grew shorter, Râkım Efendi moved the lessons and started teaching the English girls for an hour and a half in the evening right after dinner. Just like the English, Râkım was very punctual and always arrived a couple minutes before the lesson to ensure that he began on time. Both the daughters and their parents urged him many times to come an hour or so earlier in order to join them for dinner. One evening Râkım felt obliged to accept this offer and left home in time to join them for dinner at their house in Beyoğlu.

That evening, on his way from Tophane to Taksim by way of Boğazkesen Street in Firuzağa, he ran into Felâtun Bey, who was storming into a *boza* shop smeared below his waist with something that looked like a creamy drink . . . perhaps *boza* or *sahleb*? Seeing him in this state, Râkım inquired:

RÂKIM: Oh, dear Sir! What happened? I'd ask if you spilled some *boza* on your clothes, but you are just entering the boza shop!

FELÂTUN: Don't even ask! I was passing by the food shop over there. Some idiot had placed a huge plate of fish with mayonnaise sauce on the windowsill. Somehow I stumbled and when I tried to grab the windowsill, I managed to pull the whole plate down onto myself.

RÂKIM: Gosh! Thank God you didn't get cut!

FELÂTUN: Exactly! What brings you to Beyoğlu tonight?

RÂKIM: I am expected at Mr. Ziklas's house.

FELÂTUN: God bless you, brother, God bless you! You've really developed an intimacy with them.

RÂKIM: What can I do? One has to work!

FELÂTUN (*mockingly*): Right, one has to work! I am talking about the mademoiselles. They talk about you all the time! You have a knack for getting the ladies' attention. How do you do it for God's sake? Whatever I do, I can't curry favor with them! That's just the way it is.

RÂKIM: In that case let me give you some advice.

FELÂTUN: If you'd be so kind . . .

RÂKIM: Ladies like me because I never try to win their sympathy. If you do the same, you should be able to have more success.

FELÂTUN: You are just saying that, do you think you can fool me? Don't I know that you play your cards close to your chest?

RÂKIM: I don't know what you mean. Do me a favor and explain exactly how I do that.

FELÂTUN: Whatever! We'll see each other another time. With your permission, I'll go and get myself cleaned up. I walked here in this state.

Râkım also needed to hurry as he was expected to be at the English household in half an hour, so they stopped talking and went their separate ways. However, Râkım still couldn't make sense of how Felâtun managed to get the sauce all over himself at the food shop. He arrived at the English household at last and found the family waiting for him to start dinner, so quickly seated himself at the table. As soon as they finished the soup course, Mr. Ziklas ordered the cook, who was assisting the servant girl at the dinner service, to bring over the mayonnaise sauce and said, "Oh! Today our servant bought a Turkish trout, and I very much like fish dressed with mayonnaise sauce, so I ordered the cook to prepare it that way. You like it too Râkım Efendi, don't you?"

The servant girl hesitated. When Mr. Ziklas repeated his order, her face froze. When Mr. Ziklas insisted again, the panic on her face intensified, and, embarrassed, she stutteringly informed them that the sauce had spilled. Mr. Ziklas was furious! Râkım was surprised! Mr. Ziklas asked, "My dear, if it was spilled, shouldn't you have prepared a new one?" The cook felt even more embarrassed and informed him that the mayonnaise had just been spilled, leaving no time to go buy fresh eggs and lemon for a new batch.

MR. ZIKLAS: Thank goodness Felâtun Bey didn't come tonight! He is not like Râkım Efendi. We consider him a guest, and we would have been so embarrassed!

RÂKIM (*curiously*): Oh! Was Felâtun Bey also supposed to be coming?

MR. ZIKLAS: Yes! I saw him today. I asked him to come. He promised saying, "I'll certainly try my best." It got dark, night came and he still hadn't arrived, so we proceeded to sit down to dinner.

RÂKIM (*surprised and with a smile*): Since he hasn't shown up yet, it probably means that he's not coming.

SERVANT GIRL (*a Greek, in broken French*): Actually, I saw Felâtun Bey at the crossroads and he was heading in this direction.

MR. ZIKLAS: When was this?

SERVANT GIRL: As the sun was just about to set.

MR. ZIKLAS: Oh, I thought you saw him just now. So does that mean he won't be coming then, Râkım Efendi?

RÂKIM: Since he promised to come, and your servant saw him heading in this direction, surely something extraordinary must have occurred that prevented him from coming.

As Râkım responded to Mr. Ziklas, he looked at the cook out of the corner of his eye and saw that she was blushing deeply. Upon seeing this, all remaining doubt in his mind was dispelled and he knew what had really happened.

What do you think he suspected?

We told you all that was known for now. This issue will become clear in three days, so we don't have the time to elaborate on something that is still only a suspicion. In any event, they had an enjoyable dinner. After dinner, they began their lesson and finished it an hour later. It had been six months since the girls started learning Turkish. During this time, the girls had gone beyond reading and writing, and were now able to combine little sentences and phrases without any mistakes and to understand the meaning of a text if it was written clearly.

After the lesson, as Râkım was getting ready to ask permission to depart, Mr. Ziklas proposed, "Monsieur Râkım! If you don't have anything else to do right now, you could stay a while longer and have some fun. We'll have the mademoiselles play some music and sing a few songs for us." Râkım gratefully agreed to stay and both girls sat in front of the piano and played together.

Râkım, reclining on one side of the room, listened to them attentively. After singing a few more *alafranga* songs, they turned to a beautiful tune by the Armenian composer Nikogos, "O morning breeze, do not blow, my darling is asleep," whereupon Râkım became emotional. Now, would you have expected Mrs. Ziklas to ask Râkım Efendi to sing this song? In *alafranga* manners it would be inappropriate to refuse such a request, and Râkım also had sufficient musical talent, so he began singing at a low pitch, slowly tuned his voice to the piano, and finished the song.

The English liked how well he sang. Afterwards, the girls charged him with transcribing the lyrics that the poet Ziya Pasha had written for the tune. And later, as Râkım translated them into French, everyone admired the beauty of each charming verse. The girls, again with Râkım's assistance, wrote the Turkish lyrics to the song underneath the notes and later sang it in Turkish. Although they had trouble synchronizing the words with the music, they were sure to succeed with further practice.

Râkım left the English household later that evening and returned home. On the way, his mind was completely consumed thinking about Felâtun Bey's mayonnaise incident. Felâtun Bey had also been invited to the Ziklas household that night, and the servant had actually seen him enter Asmalımescit Street, but nevertheless he hadn't arrived for dinner. Râkım had also observed him with mayonnaise sauce spilled all over his clothes. And during dinner they had talked about some mayonnaise getting spilled. If one puts two and two together, one couldn't possibly reach a conclusion that would make Felâtun Bey proud. Upon arriving home, he saw that his nanny had gone to sleep due to her old age, and that only Janan was waiting for him. Gracious God! This girl was becoming more beautiful every single day! How polite, well-spoken, and full of joy she was! It was impossible for somebody not to cheer up upon seeing her! She had also learned Turkish thoroughly. She tickled people's fancy whenever she said something with that accent unique to the Circassians!

Yes, these ideas certainly crossed Râkım's mind. Definitely. But he suppressed his emotions and sighed, for he had entirely different ideas as far as Janan was concerned. It had gotten late, so while helping him undress, Janan limited herself to asking him a few questions, and he went to bed straightaway. Janan retired to her room. They both went to sleep.

Over the next few days, Râkım reflected continuously on the mayonnaise incident. The next day, when he came home, Janan gave him a letter saying, "Remember that servant who always brings notes from the foreigners? He brought it." Râkım opened the letter and realized that it was from Jan and Margaret. Here is the translation:

> Our esteemed teacher!
> Our father saw Felâtun Bey today. He complained to him that he had not shown up for dinner the other day, and asked him to come tonight for sure. Felâtun Bey promised to come. We, on the other hand, do not enjoy his presence as much as we enjoy yours. So we ask you to please come to the house sometime before dinner. We assume that you will accept our request to save your two dear students from their anguish.
>
> Margaret and Jan

Râkım was taken aback by the wording of the letter. He thought to himself, "How strange that the girls don't enjoy Felâtun Bey's presence, but that they enjoy mine. I wonder why. I haven't done anything to make them like me. I haven't thought of anything besides fulfilling my teaching duties. I wonder what Felâtun did to make them so dislike him? Did the mayonnaise incident make them suspicious perhaps? Nah! Nobody could have gotten to the bottom of it yet, could they? They are hoping that I'll rescue them, my 'two dear students,' from their anguish, huh? *Dear* students? Where did they get that idea? There is something strange going on here, but let's wait and see."

As it was Thursday, Janan's piano teacher arrived in the late afternoon. Josephine was happy to find Râkım home, and scolded him affectionately,

JOSEPHINE: Well, well, Monsieur Râkım! I'm surprised to see you. Do you ever come home?

RÂKIM: Doesn't everybody come home, Madame?

JOSEPHINE: Everybody does but you seem to be an exception. It has been months since I've last seen you!

RÂKIM: To tell you the truth, I regret how much business has kept me away from home.

JOSEPHINE: I don't care about that. Remember our deal? If a teacher isn't paid, she has the right to quit.

RÂKIM: Of course! You're quite right about that, Madame. But I trust that your humanity and compassion will permit you to forgive me.

JOSEPHINE: No way. I don't know what sort of business has kept you from having a decent conversation with me. I think you find those tomato-y English girls so attractive that you're not able to see us, your true friends.

RÂKIM: Not at all, Madame! That thought never even crossed my mind. You know me!

JOSEPHINE: Right, and I'm telling you this *because* I know you! I have every right to scold you. You come to Beyoğlu twice a week to tutor the English girls but you never stop by your friend Josephine's house to say hello, even though it's the polite thing to do.

RÂKIM: Now I agree that this has been a mistake on my part. But I made this mistake because I don't know where your house is. Honestly, Madame, you have the right to scold me. Please do so. In fact, if you really want, I shall give you a stick and let you beat me. But however you choose to punish me, please do it now so that I know I am forgiven.

JOSEPHINE: Whatever the punishment?

RÂKIM: Yes, Madame!

JOSEPHINE: Well then, I've decided on your punishment. I'll implement it when the time comes.

RÂKIM: For my part, starting tomorrow, I won't neglect my duty to stop by your house and pay my regards before I leave Beyoğlu.

After this conversation was over, Josephine told Janan, who was waiting for her:

JOSEPHINE: *Voyons. Ma petite! As-tu appris ta leçon?* (Let's see, my dear! Have you learned your lesson?)

JANAN: *Oui*, Madame (Yes, Ma'm).

RÂKIM: What's this? Is our Janan also learning French?

JOSEPHINE: If she doesn't learn French, how can I speak with her? Am I going to be forced to learn Turkish while she can learn French easily?

JANAN (*shyly*): Yes, Sir! Madame is having me learn French.

RÂKIM: Why are you blushing and complaining as if you are doing something wrong? How wonderful! You shouldn't just learn to speak French. I shall . . .

JANAN: I am not only learning to speak it, Sir, I am learning to write as well.

RÂKIM: Let me see how you write it.

Janan went to fetch her notebook. Râkım saw that her notebook had a lot of French words written in Turkish script and said that this wasn't the way to learn French. He promised that he would tutor her in French himself. It is odd that Janan, unlike Josephine, didn't seem particularly excited about this prospect.

Indeed! Janan wasn't too happy about learning French. But you know that Janan could learn something even if she wasn't inclined, faster even than those who are enthusiastic about it since she was naturally so intelligent, an intelligence which had been dormant before Râkım bought her. She was so smart! Josephine was amazed that she never had to repeat any lesson. Her quick comprehension led Josephine to grow even fonder of this poor little girl. What we are trying to say is that she would certainly learn the French lessons that Râkım began to give her that evening, as quickly and skillfully as she had learned Turkish and how to play the piano.

Oh! It has been some time since we informed you about Janan's Turkish. She started writing about this and that, and could comprehend every new book she read by herself. Râkım even started showing her some Arabic and Persian using a shortcut method.

The next day, Râkım went to Beyoğlu a little earlier as he intended to visit both Josephine and the Ziklas household. He arrived at Josephine's house, which he learned was on Posta Street, shortly before sunset. Josephine was waiting for him. After the preliminary *"Bonjour,* Madame," *"Bonjour,* Monsieur," and inquiring about each other's health, they started chatting. They spoke highly of Janan. Josephine admired Janan's acute intelligence, found her beauty to be exceptional, and was surprised that Râkım wasn't moved by her attributes even though she lived with him and was his own property.

Are we sensing some discomfort in Josephine? Yes! Although she discoursed pleasantly, there was clearly something unspoken on her mind. Meanwhile, another topic came up:

JOSEPHINE: Do you drink *rakı*, Monsieur Râkım?

RÂKIM: To be honest, Madame, I can't say either yes or no. Sometimes I do. But I'm not in the habit.

JOSEPHINE: Honestly Sir, one of the best things about this place is *rakı*. I like it very much. Let me tell you a secret. Just like the Turks, I drink *rakı* every night, but just a little! About three or four glasses.

RÂKIM: That's good, Madame. A little bit of *rakı* can be rather nice.

JOSEPHINE: Should I order some?

RÂKIM: As you wish, Madame.

Josephine called for her servant Marie and ordered some *rakı*. As it had already been prepared to be served, Marie returned with it immediately and placed it on the table in the middle of the room. They poured some into their glasses, toasted saying, "To your health!" and drank. Râkım couldn't take his eyes off the piano that was on one side of the room. Josephine noticed this and asked,

JOSEPHINE: Would you like it if I played the guitar and sang some of those so-called romance songs?

RÂKIM: I would be overjoyed!

After they drank another glass of *rakı*, Josephine picked up her guitar. She started off with an introduction to the song and proposed another glass. Râkım said that he couldn't drink that fast. Josephine drank another glass saying that everyone was free to do whatever they wished. As a result she sang the final parts of the song in a pleasant and melancholy way.

After she stopped playing, Râkım refilled only half of his glass as he wasn't used to drinking but at Josephine's request filled hers all the way up, and they toasted again. Josephine's eyes started to look different, and her earlier discomfort gave way to elation. Râkım said, "Now I understand how mistaken and foolish I've been for not pursuing our friendship. In fact, from now on I'll never make this mistake again and will even dare to give you a headache with my conversation." When he said that, Josephine rose to her feet and approached Râkım saying, "Oh! You just reminded me: I was going to give you your punishment."

RÂKIM: Is punishment still necessary, Madame? After honoring me with all these compliments, how can you punish me?

JOSEPHINE: Of course I can. There is no way I'm not punishing you for your mistake.

With that, she boldly gave him a passionate kiss. This turn of events didn't surprise Râkım because by then he had already suspected from her behavior that things were headed in that direction. After chatting for another hour, he said goodbye to Josephine and headed over to the Ziklas household. He was surprised by how his luck and destiny changed colors like a chameleon at every turn.

It's quite possible that some readers are now asking how Râkım and Josephine conversed during the hour after the aforementioned incident took place. In storytelling, some details should be left out. These details can be figured out through intuition. Let us tell you this much: when Râkım was taking leave of Josephine, she said to him, "I have now revealed my secret and expressed my love. My feelings arise from knowing that you are a man worth loving and that you have a reputation for being morally upright and honorable. You also know that I have a similar reputation to uphold in this social circle. You must understand how important it is to keep what happened a secret." Râkım thanked her, responding that he had been about to ask the same of her, and took his leave.

Look at that! Felâtun Bey was right; Râkım Efendi does play his cards close to his chest!

Yes, esteemed readers! We already told you we're not describing the manners of an angel. We're describing the true nature of a young man who knows how to protect his honor and to live decently and genuinely *alafranga*. But above all we are describing someone of our times. If you can show us a young man who could have restrained himself in Râkım's situation that night, we will add him to this story. Reasonable young men like Râkım know how to play their cards close to their chests and keep certain things under their hats. But if you are looking for the opposite sort, Felâtun Bey is the perfect example.

Now, when you look at these two young men from the moral point of view . . . How perfect! We are offering you two kinds of morality by showing you the behavior of two young men of our time. You're free to choose the one you prefer. You're also free to dislike both of them!

Fearing that he might be late for his lesson, Râkım Efendi rushed to Asmalımescit. He knocked forcefully on Mr. Ziklas's door because he'd arrived in a hurry and was still preoccupied thinking about his earlier behavior. The weather was overcast and it had already grown dark. What do you think Râkım encountered as the door opened and he entered the house? Let's see:

As soon as he stepped inside, a bulky woman hugged Râkım and squeezed him tightly. "Cruel man! Why are you late? I've been waiting for such a long time, are you going to spill mayonnaise sauce all over yourself again tonight?" she said in French.

Do you now understand that this lady was the cook and see how the mayonnaise incident must have unfolded?

Râkım didn't say a word but the cook realized what she had done and immediately begged for forgiveness. Râkım, feigning ignorance, managed to get her to admit what had really happened with the mayonnaise sauce.

She was a corpulent, buxom French woman and apparently Felâtun Bey liked her. She liked Felâtun Bey, too, both for his looks and for his money, and after only a short time they had arrived at the point where they almost "cooked it." Two nights ago Felâtun Bey accidentally knocked the mayonnaise pot down over himself while he was making love to the cook in the kitchen. There was no way he could go upstairs to join the family for dinner in that condition, so he fled from the house. The cook begged Râkım to keep this incident a secret, and he assured her that she could trust him.

Felâtun Bey hadn't arrived at the Ziklas house yet and the Ziklas family, along with some of their other friends, a couple ladies and a few men, were waiting for Râkım and Felâtun.

Felâtun Bey showed up ten minutes later. Mr. Ziklas uttered a few words to Felâtun about keeping his friends waiting but Felâtun explained that his father was very sick and that this had prevented him from coming on time. Mr. Ziklas accepted his apology.

They all sat down together at the dinner table and began to eat their soup.

MR. ZIKLAS (*to the cook*): Hopefully tonight the mayonnaise sauce hasn't been spilled.

As soon as he heard these words, Felâtun Bey glanced at Mr. Ziklas, Râkım, and the cook but was relieved when he saw no sign of suspicion in their expressions, with the exception of the cook.

RÂKIM: From now on they'll be more careful, Sir, and won't spill the mayonnaise sauce.

FELÂTUN (*to cover his embarrassment*): What happened, Sir? Did somebody spill the mayonnaise sauce one night?

MR. ZIKLAS: Yes! Last night, she spilled the mayonnaise sauce at the last minute, so we had to eat plain boiled fish.

Nothing more about the mayonnaise incident was uttered that night, and they started talking about other things. Yet, whenever Felâtun Bey glanced at the cook, she was reminded of the incident and blushed.

There isn't any need to expand on the conversation that followed at the dinner table. Except for when they started talking about what a refined and pleasant language Ottoman was and how difficult it was to teach, Jan and Margaret earned everyone's compliments by reciting Râkım Efendi's translation of the song "O morning breeze, do not blow/my darling is asleep." In the meantime, Felâtun Bey tried to demonstrate Râkım's ignorance once again and wanted Râkım to feel even more embarrassed than he himself had over the mayonnaise incident, so he asserted that the song didn't start with the verse "O morning breeze, do not blow," but rather with "O morning breeze, my brunette darling," and even went so far as to declare that brunette meant *blonde* in French.

Râkım didn't say anything to this objection; he only contented himself with a strange smile. But at the table was Baron T——, who had sufficient knowledge of Ottoman, and he started to object to Felâtun Bey and confirmed that the song should indeed start with the verse "O morning breeze, do not blow/my darling is asleep."

MARGARET: What's more, Sir, does the French word *blonde* really mean brunette? Our teacher, Râkım Efendi, translated that word as *blond* for us. I wonder if that is a mistake, too.

4. Pages 38 and 39 from the Ottoman publication of *Felâtun Bey and Râkım Efendi*. Published in 1875 by Mehmet Cevdet. Provided by the Atatürk Kitaplığı (Taksim, Istanbul).

BARON T: No, no, my dear! Your teacher translated it very nicely; *blonde* means blond in Turkish. Brunette can be translated to French as *brun*.

As these words were exchanged, Felâtun Bey grew increasingly embarrassed, so Râkım attempted to change the subject to shield him.

After dinner, at the guests' request, Margaret and Jan played the "O morning breeze" song together on the piano and sang along to it. As they had sung it at least fifteen times in the last three days, they performed so well that even Felâtun Bey found himself enjoying it. Then they started playing a polka with some guests pairing up to dance. This kind of entertainment at such gatherings was common for those in the *alafranga* world. Mrs. Ziklas asked Râkım why he wasn't dancing, to which Râkım apologized, saying that although he could do the quadrille and other dances, dancing the polka and the waltz made him dizzy. Felâtun Bey, on the other hand, had been begging Margaret for the last five minutes to dance with him just once. Margaret, unable to disoblige Felâtun Bey, somehow managed to get up from her seat. Even though Jan was left alone in front of the piano, she still maintained the tempo. To be honest, we can't criticize Felâtun Bey's dancing. His pants were so tight that he was forced to dance straight as a ramrod and couldn't bend.

However, during the dance, he accidently tread on Margaret's feet and panicked. While trying to handle this situation, he made a sudden move that was followed by a ripping sound that came from behind him.

Don't get the wrong idea! That's not what it was. It was nothing other than the thorough splitting of his very tight black pants. His jacket was so short that it didn't cover the rip, so the hole in his pants was obvious. Thank heavens he was wearing underwear that night. Felâtun Bey had a habit of not wearing underwear when he attended such important gatherings, in order not to impede the smoothness of his pants, as he believed that this was the *alafranga* way. If he had adhered to this convention tonight, then the problem would have become even more obvious. Although it was tactless, nobody could refrain from laughing when they saw it. Felâtun ran off before he could even bid them adieu.

There is nothing else to report about that night's incidents—only that when Râkım found his students Jan and Margaret alone in one corner, he asked them why they disliked Felâtun Bey. In addition to their mention of this in the note they had sent, Râkım also observed Margaret's reluctance to dance with Felâtun that night.

JAN: Felâtun Bey is not a parlor gentleman.

MARGARET: He would be just right for a coffeehouse.

RÂKIM: Why do you think that Madame? He is young, smart, alert, and knowledgeable.

MARGARET: Come on now! What good is a young, handsome man if he doesn't know his own alphabet and can't even get the beginning of a song right?

JAN: That's not the real problem, Sir. I said he's not a parlor gentleman. What Margaret said explains it all. He's a coffeehouse man, so he assumes that the girls he encounters in the parlor are the same as the girls he sees in the coffeehouses.

RÂKIM: He's still young.

MARGARET: Surely he's older than you.

Chapter 5

OH RÂKIM! He must have realized that Felâtun Bey had been trying to embarrass him, so one would expect that he'd enjoy seeing how Felâtun Bey ended up embarrassing himself; but to the contrary Râkım felt saddened by this as he made his way back home in a coach. He was preoccupied with thoughts concerning Felâtun's embarrassment as he neared home. The sound of Janan playing the piano came from an open window and stirred him from this pensive state of mind. He dismissed the coachman and knocked on the door thinking, "This poor girl! She is still waiting. When I see her face now, my emotions will swell up again. I wonder why she has such an effect on me. I don't know what kind of love I have for her. It's not like what Josephine described. It is not the way I described it, I mean, she is neither like my sister nor my beloved! This is a whole different thing. Let this be another kind of love." As soon as he knocked on the door, the sound of the piano ceased and he heard Janan's footsteps coming toward him. She opened the door.

RÂKIM: So you haven't gone to bed yet, Janan!

JANAN: I was waiting for you, Sir. Nanny is sleeping.

RÂKIM: Oh, so weren't you disturbing her by playing the piano?

JANAN: She gave me permission, Sir. She wanted me to play.

RÂKIM: Your piano teacher sends her regards. I saw her tonight.

JANAN: Oh! I am very glad to hear it. She was a bit resentful.

RÂKIM: She won't be anymore!

As he said these words, Râkım was filled with a thousand incompatible emotions including shame, regret, enthusiasm, affection, fear, and terror.

Nevertheless, he suppressed all of these sentiments and went to his room. Janan helped him undress.

RÂKIM: So, do you like your teacher, Janan?

JANAN: To be honest Sir, I like her very much. She is such a smart and skillful woman.

RÂKIM: She likes you, too. In fact she is offering these lessons more for your sake than mine.

JANAN: God bless her.

After telling Janan a little more about his day, the conversation arrived at this point:

RÂKIM: Are you getting bored Janan?

JANAN: No, Sir! Why should I?

RÂKIM: No, I mean to say, would you like to go on an outing?

JANAN: How should I know, Sir? You know better. Nanny knows the world outside better.

RÂKIM: If you wanted to go out, wouldn't Nanny take you if you asked her?

JANAN: She would, Sir. Why wouldn't she? But I don't really want that. There's no need. I have thousands of things to amuse myself with here. I have my books, my writing, and my piano. I'm very comfortable, Sir. I have my garden, too. Nanny got me a little shovel and a small tin watering can from the market in Salıpazarı. I enjoy working in the garden.

RÂKIM (*patting her on the back*): Good for you, Janan!

What do you think about this? You know what, the girl was thunderstruck! It was evident in her blushing. It was obvious that Râkım didn't want to send the girl to her room. Quite possibly, the girl didn't want to go either. Yet, it was very late, so they retired to their rooms and went to sleep. Probably neither of them was able to fall asleep for quite a while.

As you might have realized from the way we've been telling this story, Râkım's thoughts had never been stimulated by such emotions until now, when his emotions were awakened passionately by Josephine, to some degree by Janan, and to a degree that he couldn't quite determine by the English girls. However, don't think that he started neglecting his work. Râkım never grew tired of his various occupations. He'd still go to those grand houses to do their writing, and he continued earning the income God bestowed on him. Râkım was nowhere near to being tightfisted, so much so that he spent whatever he earned on his house, his nanny, and Janan, and when he had extra income, he considered wasting it inappropriate, so he gave it to his nanny, who put it aside.

If you really want to understand the way Râkım lived, look at the way Janan lived.

As we said from the beginning, whenever a new trend appeared in Istanbul, Janan was always one of the first to dress accordingly. Additionally, Janan's closet had the best artificial flowers, and her jewelry box didn't lack a couple of diamond brooches, earrings, and rings. Not a week went by when Râkım didn't give Janan eighty or a hundred kuruş in the form of gold or silver coins. But what could Janan do with all this money? She didn't go out, and she didn't need anything else. She gave all the money to Nanny, who put it aside, and after accumulating a certain amount, she'd ask Râkım Efendi to buy a ring, a watch, or a bracelet—in short, some kind of jewelry for Janan. Why should we mince words? We can't call her a gentleman's wife because she wasn't married, but poor Janan was vouchsafed an even better life.

Given this, there's no need to ask how Râkım lived. We've already established how he lived. He'd go to Beyoğlu twice a week, visit Josephine, and later teach the English girls with honor and decorum. In addition, if Josephine were to find Râkım at home on her weekly visits, they would spend time talking about this and that, making quips and jokes.

Here you are. This is how things continued until spring. However, there are some other stories that need to be told and we feel obliged to recount them.

In the meantime, Felâtun Bey's father, Mustafa Meraki Efendi, died a natural death after suffering for about fifteen days from the sickness his son had mentioned. May he rest in peace. His son Felâtun Bey could fend for himself as he was after all a man, while Meraki's poor daughter Mihriban Hanım was still very young.

Oh come on! You shouldn't consider them orphans; their family had a monthly income of twenty thousand kuruş!

Don't say such things, ladies and gentlemen. At the very least, one can't help but feel pity for them.

There was also the fact that Felâtun Bey hadn't been seen in the Ziklas household for some time. In fact, the French cook had been replaced. Why, you ask? Râkım Efendi learned the reason from the English girls. That is to say:

Râkım was chatting with the girls and their parents one night after the lesson. Somehow he led the conversation around to Felâtun Bey and said that he hadn't seen Felâtun Bey for quite some time.

MRS. ZIKLAS: Râkım Efendi! I'd like to prohibit you and my children from uttering that man's name. The children have already been prohibited anyway!

RÂKIM (*very uneasily*): May I ask the reason, Madame?

MR. ZIKLAS: No, Sir. You may not! In fact, I'm pleased that you haven't seen him recently. This means that you were only accustomed to seeing him here.

RÂKIM: Yes, Sir!

MR. ZIKLAS: Well that's that then! God knows, we are very content with your honor, decorum and morals and we are just as pleased with your teaching.

RÂKIM: I am grateful for your kindness, Sir.

As these words were exchanged between Râkım and the parents, the girls hung their heads and could not even raise their eyebrows. The conversation ended and it was time for Râkım to head home. He suspected from the cook's disappearance that the problem must be related to the mayonnaise incident; however, there was no way to confirm this until the next lesson, which he therefore anticipated eagerly.

Finally, that day came. Râkım arrived at the Ziklas household earlier than usual and attempted to have the girls satisfy his curiosity before starting the lesson. They were even able to conduct the conversation in Turkish. The girls' Turkish was sufficiently advanced to allow them to have this conversation.

RÂKIM: For God's sake, ladies, I am about to burst with curiosity! What happened to Felâtun Bey?

JAN: Didn't I tell you that he wasn't a parlor man?

MARGARET: And didn't I tell you that he was a coffeehouse man?

RÂKIM: Never mind! I'd like to know exactly what happened.

MARGARET: It's so inappropriate that I can't bring myself to say it.

JAN: Me neither.

RÂKIM: Oh, come on! Why not? That's not possible. You can't leave me in the dark about this. It would sadden me if you didn't view me as a confidant after all this time.

MARGARET: This is not something that a polite person can talk about but since I can't refuse your request, I will just say it despite my embarrassment. He came here a few nights ago and stayed for dinner. But he wasn't received as a formal guest anymore and we don't particularly enjoy his company, so we occupied ourselves with our studies. I don't know exactly how it happened, but at some point when he was coming into the house, he ran into my mother in the corridor. He did not recognize her, or rather, he mistook her for our cook, so he hugged her and said, "Oh sweetie! Are you going to spill the mayonnaise all over me again? You almost made a fool of me in front of Râkım and the others!" Hearing this, my mother yelled "Oh my!" When Felâtun Bey realized what was going on, he ran into the living room, and without even having the chance to pick up his coat and fez, dashed out into the street in embarrassment. My mother immediately came into the living room. She threw his fez and coat out the window into the street. She then recounted the whole story to my father. Apparently that night when the mayonnaise was spilled . . .

RÂKIM: I got it, Madame, I got it! It was really disgraceful of him. Let's cut this chitchat or your parents might have second thoughts about me.

JAN: No, Sir! They won't have any suspicions concerning you. They have complete trust in you.

There, this is really how the whole mayonnaise issue came to a conclusion. As Jan said, both Mr. and Mrs. Ziklas indeed had complete trust in Râkım. Both of them loved Râkım like a son or a brother. This was because Râkım encountered all kinds of men and women in that household—in fact, he also met some very independent French ladies—but he still never lost any of his decorum in their presence.

It's often said that the theater is the best place to discover the true personality of a young man. Those who saw Felâtun Bey at a theater never noticed him entering the married ladies' box to greet them. He was always busy laughing in the boxes of unattended women or those who treated every man as their owner. Râkım, on the other hand, would buy his ticket, enter the theater, and survey the people in the boxes. Whenever he stopped by the boxes of nobles like G—— Bey to greet them, they would offer him a seat saying, "Our magnificent son, Râkım Efendi, here you are! There is always a place for you here." He would typically accept the first offer of a seat and during intermission would ask permission to greet other families in other boxes. When he went around to pay his respects, the people he was seated with would say, "What a composed young man! He doesn't have any bad habits like drinking or gambling! Honestly, he behaves as well as a girl." In fact, for a few days afterwards, families continued to talk about Râkım this way. What we mean to say is that Mr. and Mrs. Ziklas were amongst those who both uttered and heard such compliments about Râkım.

Let us tell you about something that happened before the arrival of spring: One night, toward the end of the winter, Râkım went to visit Josephine before going to the English household. As they had been on familiar terms for quite some time, Josephine leapt for joy upon seeing him. They asked after each other's well-being, and she broached a topic. Her face was crestfallen:

JOSEPHINE: Monsieur Râkım! Do you have any doubts about my friendship?

RÂKIM: How could I have any doubts?

JOSEPHINE: No, no, I'm not joking. Do you consider me to be your mistress?

RÂKIM: Why are you saying such things?

JOSEPHINE: I will explain why. To begin with, we should acknowledge that we don't just love each other amorously; we love each other like true friends. And we care sincerely about each other.

RÂKIM: Okay, okay, I agree. Let's see if I understand this correctly. That's certainly how I feel about our friendship, and I'm pleased if that's how you feel, too.

JOSEPHINE: Okay now, I have something to tell you . . . but wait a minute . . . let me put it this way; I want to see how you'll react. Let's say there was a customer interested in purchasing Janan.

RÂKIM: It could happen.

JOSEPHINE: But you don't know the kind of customer I'm talking about.

RÂKIM: You are trying to say he's rich, is that right?

JOSEPHINE: He is ready to pay 1,500 Ottoman liras immediately. As you know, this corresponds to 34,500 francs. That's a lot of money.

RÂKIM: Yes! I have enough math to multiply 1,500 by twenty-three. But tell me . . . who is this customer?

JOSEPHINE: You know, that gentleman, —— Bey. What do you think? Would you accept that offer?

RÂKIM: How did he learn about my female slave?

JOSEPHINE: From me. Although I have been teaching his female slaves for seven or eight months just like I've been teaching Janan, they haven't learned anything. The other day their master started to reproach me on their lack of progress. I told him about Janan. I said, "You should be happy if your girls could learn as much Turkish, French, piano, reading, and writing in eight years as she learned in eight months." So, he sent his treasurer the next morning to examine Janan surreptitiously. He even thought that what I said about Janan was an understatement. When I went there yesterday, he confirmed my thoughts and expressed great enthusiasm about her French and piano skills. What I mean is, he asked me to sound you out to see if you'd sell her for 1,500 liras.

RÂKIM: Not a bad deal, eh? Selling the female slave that I bought for a hundred gold coins for 1,500 liras.

JOSEPHINE: He was particularly taken with her beauty. In fact, his treasurer even said to him, "Sir, she's not a female slave, she's a dignified lady." In any case, are you willing to sell Janan?

RÂKIM: It's not for me to decide.

JOSEPHINE: Well, whose decision is it?

RÂKIM: Janan herself.

JOSEPHINE: What are you saying?

RÂKIM: What I'm saying is that I've never given Janan a reason to suppose that she might become my concubine or wife. She is a woman. Of course she will want a husband for herself one day. If she is hoping to get another master to accept her as a concubine in the future, then I'll sell her. She'll already have a sizeable fortune from her jewelry and possessions. Would it be so terrible if we added the 1,500 liras to that and made Janan a lady with 2,000 liras?

JOSEPHINE: My! Will you really let Janan keep the 1,500 liras as well?

RÂKIM: What, should I pocket the money myself? Do you think I'm that greedy and hardhearted? How could I pocket the price of her freedom?

JOSEPHINE: You mean, you're not thinking of selling her?

RÂKIM: I already told you what I think!

JOSEPHINE: Are you saying that 1,500 liras isn't enough to separate you from Janan?

RÂKIM: Indeed, it wouldn't be enough to separate me from her. However, if it's enough for Janan, then I won't oppose it.

JOSEPHINE: Bravo, Râkım! Bravo young man! My God, I hadn't dared hope that you'd say this!

Josephine hugged Râkım and kissed him on his eyes, forehead, and cheeks.

JOSEPHINE: I assure you that this money won't be enough to make Janan want to leave you. She's so noticeably fond of you. This level of affection is rare indeed. I've sounded her out before and clearly her little heart is filled with affection for you.

RÂKIM: Didn't you expect this from me?

JOSEPHINE: In all honesty, I did not.

RÂKIM: Frankly, I didn't expect this from you, either.

JOSEPHINE: What do you mean?

RÂKIM: Because I thought you were competing against Janan.

JOSEPHINE (jokingly): Come off it, you silly man!

RÂKIM: Why? You mean you don't love me?

JOSEPHINE: Let me repeat again: Silly man!

RÂKIM: Why? For God's sake, now you're making me sad. When I thought you loved me . . .

JOSEPHINE: You crazy man, who doesn't love you? I should content myself with the thought that I gained your affection. But am I worthy of becoming your life companion? I'm nearly forty years old while you are a young man of only twenty-five. If I had lived in this country and married when I was fifteen, I'd now have a son your age.

RÂKIM: No, you're worthier even than becoming my . . .

JOSEPHINE: Shush! I won't listen to such unseemly talk. If you're going to be anything, then be my friend. Be my companion. Janan is the only woman in this world worthy of you. Poor little girl! How cute . . . and that doleful face, that melancholy attitude! Râkım! Râkım! Did you really think that I was one of those theater whores? I have a soul, a soul filled with emotions. I love Janan more than you do. Even if I didn't, I wouldn't hold back from speaking the truth. I won't consider you a man if you leave this girl dejected.

RÂKIM (surprised): My God, this is strange indeed! I've never met a woman like you.

JOSEPHINE: Well you have now. The next time I go to that gentleman's house, I'll tell him that his offer has been . . . rejected. Right?

RÂKIM: For my part, yes.

JOSEPHINE: That's also true for Janan . . . Her happiness is my own.

Unable to fathom Josephine's attitude, Râkım left Posta Street bewildered. He arrived in Asmalımescit. Although he wasn't able to comprehend Josephine's behavior, he recognized a great compassion, righteousness, and love for both Janan and himself in her. Râkım arrived at the Ziklas household in Asmalımescit. After he knocked on the door and entered, Râkım found the two sisters waiting for him. Surprised at the absence of their parents, he felt obliged to ask:

RÂKIM: I don't see your parents, Mr. and Mrs. Ziklas.

MARGARET: They're not here tonight.

RÂKIM: Odd! You're alone then. Why didn't they take you with them?

MARGARET and JAN: Because they knew you were coming.

RÂKIM: Now, this makes me sad. I could've come and tutored you tomorrow. Why did you deny yourselves this pleasure?

JAN: We can also enjoy ourselves in your company.

RÂKIM: Sure, but it'd be better if you were with your mother.

MARGARET: They aren't far; they are over at Monsieur ——'s soirée. We could go there after dinner if you wanted. However, we'd rather stay here.

RÂKIM: As you wish.

JAN (suggestively): If you don't like us, then . . .

RÂKIM: You must be kidding me! I love you like sisters.

MARGARET: And we love you as a brother.

RÂKIM: Thank you, ladies. I would never tire of your company even after a lifetime. Don't you know that by now?

JAN: We feel the same way about you.

They sat down and ate dinner. After leaving the dinner table, they occupied themselves with their lessons for an hour. That night their lesson was dedicated exclusively to the translation of some songs and love poems. Râkım was always surprised how much the girls enjoyed Ottoman poetry. The poetic and amorous manner with which the girls recited these poems visibly moved their listeners. They discussed the poems together:

JAN: English poetry never makes one thirsty for love. I used to like French poetry more but now that I've learned Turkish, I've given up on French poetry as well.

MARGARET: Me too. What is a poem good for if it doesn't ignite a fire in you?

RÂKIM: What are you saying? I've never heard you talk this way before.

MARGARET: What way do you mean?

RÂKIM: About poems igniting a fire and all. Who is the source of these feelings?

JAN: I don't know what you mean, Râkım Efendi! Are we made of wood?

RÂKIM: That's all good. But there is a time for everything my dear. As your teacher, I suppose I reserve the right to warn you that it's not the right time to cultivate such thoughts yet.

JAN: Indeed, we concede you the right to warn us.

MARGARET: We even welcome it, and we assure you that we'll never take advantage of your concern.

RÂKIM (*with a little smile after thinking for a while*): Take advantage?

JAN: Why did you laugh for God's sake?

RÂKIM: No reason.

JAN: Oh, come on! You laughed for a reason. Don't keep it from us. Don't you consider us your sisters?

RÂKIM: I do, I do, but . . .

MARGARET: But what?

RÂKIM: Since you are so enthusiastic about poetry . . . I could show you some Persian poems and even translate some of the better Ottoman ones; however, I fear that you might take advantage of this much independence.

After the girls secured Râkım's consent, they showed signs of happiness
to the point of embracing him, and said:

JAN: Don't you trust our good morals?

RÂKIM: Absolutely!

MARGARET: Do we have to prove ourselves to you again?

RÂKIM: No! I am confident of your good morals. But girls who are so passionate
about poetry can't easily tolerate the overflow of poetic emotions.

JAN: We assure you that we won't reveal our emotions to anyone.

RÂKIM: All right then, listen.

Râkim started reading the following poem by Hafez:

> You whose visage brightens the light of my eyes
> No eye in this world has seen any eye more pleasant than your languid
> eye
>
> The world has never shown forth, and God not created
> One precious as you, charming head to toe
>
> Aiming to spill the lovers' blood, her eyebrow and laughing eyes
> At times wait in ambush, at times pull taut the bow
>
> Constant smoke from the burning in my heart swirls around my head
> How long will I, like sandalwood smolder in the fire
>
> If you place your lips on my lips, I'll receive eternal life
> At the moment I give up the sweet ghost through my lips

Those who know this poem will recognize that Râkım omitted a
few of its couplets. We don't know why he did this. It's possible that he
couldn't remember those couplets off the top of his head, or maybe he
thought that it wasn't the right time or place for their utterance. As
he read, he employed a fine Shiraz accent, turning the Persian language
around in his mouth as if he were savoring candy. Although the girls
weren't able to comprehend the meaning yet, they admired the sweet-
ness of the pronunciation when Râkım translated the poem and con-
veyed its meaning. The girls, whose amorous feelings had already been
awakened, were intoxicated.

To acquaint our readers with the particular interpretation of the poem that Râkım offered the girls, we replicate it as follows:

"Don't you see that my eyes are glittering with happiness and profuse relief? / But don't attribute its reason to something else. The brightness of my eye's light is only a radiance caused by the reflection of the light of your bright face / Have you ever picked up the mirror to stare at your own beauty and paid particular attention to the beauty of your eyes? The eyes of the whole universe have not seen such ecstatic eyes / If your own eyes lack the ability to see your own beauty, then let me tell you. No one in the whole world has been able to attest to the beauty head-to-toe of a coquette like you. In fact, God has not created such a body yet / Are you not going to ask about the influence staring at you has on us? We are shaking like a leaf before your eyes and eyebrows / While your ecstatic eyes lay in ambush, your brutal eyebrows have drawn their bows to make an attempt on the lover's life. Yet, you take delight in our tearful entreaties and our mournful sighs / We are always suffused with the smoke emanating from our burning bosoms; let us keep on burning just like an aloe tree to obtain the natural scent of this fragrant smoke / I have fallen sick with the disease of your love. I have become bed-ridden. See, there is no hope left for the continuation of my life / At this moment when my sweet life has come all the way up to my lips, if you put your lips on mine, there, I will find eternal life. Otherwise, I will be wracked by pain and perish."

Just as the girls finished noting down Râkım's French translation of the poem, their parents returned. Mr. Ziklas, pleased at finding them seated at the writing desk, said:

MR. ZIKLAS: See, my son, this is exactly what I'd expect from appreciative and well-mannered men. It appears that you spent three or four hours this evening studying.

JAN: Yes, dear father.

MRS. ZIKLAS: Truthfully, a man like Râkım is hard to find.

RÂKIM: You honor me with your compliments, Madame!

MR. ZIKLAS: Shall we drink a glass of punch?

RÂKIM: I wish you'd excuse me since Salıpazarı is rather far away, as you know, Sir!

MR. ZIKLAS: Yes, you live in Salıpazarı. You are right; it *is* quite far away, dear Râkım Efendi! You've never invited us to your house. We've never seen an *alaturka* house.

GIRLS: Oh my God, dear father. We want to see his house, too. I wonder how many books he has!

MRS. ZIKLAS: Books are these girls' passion!

MR. ZIKLAS: That's right, my dear! They got these thoughts from Râkım Efendi. Seriously Râkım Efendi, bring us to your house one day.

RÂKIM: Certainly, Sir! I'd be delighted! Whenever you want. However, it would be nice if you could wait until the arrival of spring. This way, you could see my little garden in its prettiest season.

GIRLS: What do you know, he has a garden too!

MRS. ZIKLAS: Okay, then. You decide when the time is right.

MR. ZIKLAS: I'm sure Râkım Efendi will choose a suitable time. We can take a boat trip while we're there as well.

EVERYBODY: Perfect!

After these words were exchanged, Râkım said goodbye to everyone and took his leave. He decided to walk back home to take advantage of the beauty of the full moon, and began to make his way down Kumbaracı Yokuşu Street.

Chapter 6

DID ANY OTHER INCIDENTS take place before the arrival of spring besides the ones recounted above in the fifth chapter?

Undoubtedly! In fact, more things happened to Râkım on that strange night. His mind was so preoccupied, thinking both about Josephine's peculiar behavior and the amorousness he spotted in the girls, that coming from Tophane he went straight past his house, through Fındıklı, and barely managed to collect himself by the time he neared Kabataş.

How strange! What was the reason for his pensiveness?

We already told you! It was a combination of Janan's situation, Josephine's behavior, and the English girls' attitude. Actually, Râkım knew Josephine to be a very benevolent, well-mannered, and polite lady. However, due to the amorous exchange that had taken place between them, he calculated that Josephine wouldn't feel the way she claimed to feel about Janan. In fact, although for some time he had been thinking, "She's right after all. Our exchange is only a way of satisfying each other's needs," he couldn't really judge her conduct and said to himself, "No, this woman used to love me, and I used to love her. Not *used to*, she still loves me, and I love her. Josephine is a woman of forty but she's not one of those beauties that can be discarded like that. Everyone could love her because of her sweet stature, beautiful manners, and polite attitude. All very well, but . . . No. Surely . . ."

As for the English girls . . . their languid blue eyes were looking increasingly different, and especially tonight while he recited the poem from Hafez, he noticed their dreamy eyes and swollen chests. "There is no doubt that some amorous feelings have arisen in these girls. Obviously they have started feeling the need to love and be loved, but I wonder whom they were sighing for . . . Oh, I really want to be their confidant. I wish I knew whom they were sighing for. If I only saw them somewhere, with the men they love . . . How delightful, how pleasant it is to see lover and beloved together," Râkım thought as he forced his mind to ponder the veiled aspects of the matter. Most particularly when the thought of Janan crossed his mind . . .

After pulling himself together near Kabataş, he returned home and knocked on the door. Janan was a bit late opening the door and it was clear that the poor girl had already fallen asleep. She was slow to respond but she opened the door before Râkım had to knock a second time. We can't describe how beautiful and appealing she looked with her sleepy and languid eyes dazzled by the light of the candlestick in her hand. Râkım nearly lost himself and desired to bury his head against this girl's chest, now fully visible in her nightdress, and smell her scent. But he hurriedly shook that off and regained his self-possession.

They went upstairs. Râkım changed into his nightclothes and lay down on the living room couch. Janan busied herself with folding his clothes. In the meantime, Râkım began speaking in a trembling voice:

RÂKIM: Dear Janan! I suppose you won't be much use around here anymore.
JANAN (*nearly jumping out of her skin with apprehension*): Excuse me, Sir?
RÂKIM: Well, there is a buyer interested in you, my dear.

Oh poor girl! Is there any way of describing how it feels to love a beauty like this? You can't love them without your heart breaking. The compassion and affection of such girls bring tears to a man's eyes. When she heard her master speak, poor Janan couldn't even let go of the clothes in her hands and started stuttering in surprise:

JANAN: T . . . t . . . th . . . there . . . is a b . . . buyer interested in me?
RÂKIM: Yes, and a very wealthy one, indeed! He's offering 1,500 gold coins for you!

Râkım blinked rapidly to try to hold back the tears welling in his eyes.

JANAN (*with growing apprehension*): That's a lot of money, isn't it, Sir?
RÂKIM: Of course it's a lot of money.

JANAN (*alarmed*): Are you going to sell me, Sir?

RÂKIM: What do you say about it?

JANAN (*turning red in the face*): I am your property, Sir. You know best.

RÂKIM (*trying to swallow the bitter emotions swelling inside of him*): I would like to know what you think.

JANAN (*with watery eyes, red nose, and trembling lips*): What can I say, Sir? You need money. If you got 1,500 gold coins, you could buy fifteen Janans like me.

As Janan uttered these words, Râkım attempted to contain his growing emotions but failed, and they spilled from his eyes. Upon seeing this, Janan couldn't prevent the heavy flood of tears from cascading from the wellspring of her eyes. Poor Janan's pain was clearly visible from her expression. It was also painful for Râkım but this pain was infused with great pleasure. Not everyone can appreciate this pleasure. Only sympathetic people can. You can only appreciate it if you haven't spent your life like a piece of insensitive wood, and if you've tasted the pleasure that comes along with sweet tears. Râkım pursued the conversation:

RÂKIM: No, you misunderstood me, Janan.

JANAN (*with a glimmer of happiness in her face*): Are you not going to sell me then, Sir?

RÂKIM: No, I *will* sell you.

JANAN: (*with a pain more intense than the one she felt before*): You know best, Sir.

RÂKIM: But do you know how I'll sell you? I will give you all of your clothes, jewelry, and the 1,500 gold coins that they are paying for you. You'll be a rich lady with these. How does that sound, do you agree?

As soon as she heard this, Janan dropped the clothes she was carrying and threw herself into her master's arms in astonishment, "I want neither the 1,500 gold coins nor the clothes, nor the jewelry! I want you, Sir, you. I shall be your slave, your servant. That would be enough to make me happy." She started kissing Râkım's feet.

RÂKIM (*barely maintaining a hold over himself*): All right, but my dear Janan, you can't remain like this forever. You are young, beautiful, intelligent, skillful, and wherever you go, you could easily become a concubine. Now that you have the means to become rich, what good am I to you?

JANAN (*crying her eyes out*): I don't want to, Sir, I don't want to. I don't need to become a concubine or rich. Let me be a servant at your house, a piece of ash in your oven . . . Let me be your slave.

RÂKIM: No, you shall be my sister. However . . .

JANAN: I am incapable of showing my gratitude for the blissful life I have at your house.

RÂKIM: But you didn't pay attention to what I said. Let me repeat, I am asking you to be my sister.

JANAN: I did pay attention, Sir. I also understood what you meant. I don't want to lie; I won't be your sister.

RÂKIM: You won't be my sister?

JANAN: I won't, Sir.

RÂKIM: Why is that?

JANAN (*with a color that was not quite red, nor purple, nor black—in short, that resembled nothing else*): I won't, Sir. I won't be your sister. Being your sister wouldn't give me the pleasure I get from being your slave. I am happy with my current condition, I assure you. If you show some compassion and don't sell me to make some money, I'll kiss your feet with gratitude, Sir. Leave me in my current condition. Whenever you call my name "Janan," I feel on top of the world. If you were to start calling me "my sister," I wouldn't experience the same pleasure in my soul. Please don't make me say more, Sir. I've told you everything already! If you want to sell me, I couldn't find it in my heart to keep you from a profit of 1,400 gold coins.

As their exchange arrived at this point, Râkım couldn't battle any of the dreams and thoughts that were attacking his brain, and he hugged the girl in defeat:

RÂKIM: I won't sell you, my dear Janan, I won't. You're more valuable to me than anything else in the whole world. Let them keep their millions of gold coins. You are enough for me. However, I am upset that you didn't accept the offer to be my sister.

JANAN (*without abandoning her decorum and pride while she was in her master's arms, and then slowly removing herself from them*): I said I wouldn't accept the offer to be your sister. I said I am content with the way I've lived until now. I feel even more content now that you have given me this assurance. For you, I'll still be the Janan that I was an hour ago. It's my greatest honor to carry out any orders that you give me. May you live long, Sir, may you live long so that I can continue to be satisfied with seeing your face while you're asleep. Please excuse me now while I retire to my room.

After saying this and observing only silence on the part of her master, she slowly retired to her room and threw herself onto her bed.

Oh! How did Râkım get through the night?

Now, this deserves some thought. Over and over he'd jump out of his bed after half an hour of frantic pensiveness and say, "This is crazy! Who can prevent me? She doesn't need to be my property. See, the girl didn't accept the offer to be my sister and . . ." Saying this, his desires would return, yet he would dive into that deep state of contemplation again and go back to bed with a strange bitterness, thinking, "No! I need to be patient! There is no need to hurry! There, she's sleeping in my house. Isn't she mine any time? The regret that comes from haste is irreparable." He made it through to morning in this anguished state.

Would you call this madness or foolishness?

We wouldn't consider it either of these. The happiness of union with a beloved comes with the sorrow of separation. There are many people who know this but among those, far fewer who can truly appreciate this unique pleasure.

Have you ever had to constrain yourself and tasted the deprivation, the separation from a girl right beside you, a girl who has committed herself to you as your slave, and even your property? If so, you wouldn't call Râkım a lunatic or a fool. If not, you're free to call him either a lunatic or a fool.

Do you know this thing called passion? It's filthy. Really filthy. When that imagined spirit of pure love is stained with filthy passion, its pleasure fades away. In fact, at such times, ambition and greed draw a curtain over the eye, obscuring the stain.

Esteemed readers! Those sweet dreams that come from the sorrow and deprivation of separation and union alike . . . oh, how long they endure! One must remember, however, that the veneration of passion is fleeting. It consists only of a trance and a stupor followed by something best described as a sickness that lasts only seconds. If one were to yearn for their beloved for forty years, the taste of that love would persist for forty years. That man would live those forty years lively and youthfully. However, if he were to live united with his beloved for forty years, the satiation would quench his ardor and age him.

Very well, but does this sophisticated reasoning apply to Râkım who was in Josephine's arms, in her embrace, only four hours ago?

If not to Râkım, then who? You need to think carefully about those previous four hours. Did he have this sultan-of-love attitude at that time? Let's see what happened the next day.

All right! So what happened the next day?

What would you expect? Râkım woke up early in the morning and proceeded directly to Josephine's house in Beyoğlu. He found her asleep. Without offering any greeting, he said:

RÂKIM: Madame, what were you telling me last night?

JOSEPHINE: How can I remember? I told you a thousand things.

RÂKIM: Didn't you say, "Don't consider me your mistress, but instead regard me as a friend."

JOSEPHINE: Yes, I did say that.

RÂKIM: If that's the case, then rest assured, from now on I'll regard you as a friend, a sister, a mother, or whatever you want.

JOSEPHINE (*with a mixture of happiness and sadness*): I'm afraid what I said would happen, happened.

RÂKIM: Last night Janan burned me furiously with her love . . .

Râkım started to tell her about the previous night but he sounded so scorched with emotion that even Josephine was anguished.

JOSEPHINE: I am very happy to hear this even though it goes against my own interests.

RÂKIM (*throws himself at her feet*): I swear that I shall never forget the taste of the time I spent with you till the last breath I take. My friendship will continue until the end of time. I beg you, please don't deprive me of the pleasure I began to taste last night.

JOSEPHINE: You're crazy, you're a lunatic, you're cruel and you're a traitor!

RÂKIM: To what do I owe this scolding?

JOSEPHINE: To your inability to maintain both of your relationships at the same time.

RÂKIM: But Josephine! Please have mercy! This is more than I can tolerate.

JOSEPHINE: I won't press you now. I see that you are burning with an intense and potent fire. You will end up in my arms again eventually. But I'd like to give you the good news: You resurrected poor Janan last night. Believe me, all the tears she shed flowed from her eyes with special delight. Ah Janan, poor little girl, even if you had taken my life away, I wouldn't be sorry. You have the right to Râkım. You deserve him more than I do.

If we recount one more event, we'll finish relating the incidents that took place before spring. Here is what happened:

It had been a week since somebody had offered to buy Janan when Râkım ran into Felâtun Bey in Taksim. Old acquaintances never disappear.

RÂKIM (*innocently*): Hello Sir, how have you been?

FELÂTUN: Don't ask, my friend. I am grateful to be over with this *deuil*, I mean, mourning. As you know, the *alafranga* way of life requires that one mourn one's father. I've been dressed in soot-black from head to toe.

RÂKIM: Yes! That practice is *alafranga*; however, we—I mean, the Turks—aren't obliged to comply with this custom. Commemorating the dead on Fridays by reciting the thirty-sixth Quranic verse, *Yasin-i Sherif* . . .

FELÂTUN: That's right, but they never leave me alone!

RÂKIM: Who's meddling in your business?

FELÂTUN: Who, you ask? Oh, my friend! Don't ask, I'm in big trouble.

RÂKIM: Oh, dear!

FELÂTUN: Trouble, but sweet trouble. My heart is occupied with the love of a sweet little actress.

RÂKIM: Is this sweet little actress the one making you mourn?

FELÂTUN: Yes! Poor little girl! She is mourning my father's death more than I am.

RÂKIM: How strange!

FELÂTUN: Yes! She is a very strange girl. How she mourns! She even insisted on buying black dinner plates. She doesn't wear anything but black in the theater. If she could, she'd cover the sun and the stars in the sky with black tulle fabric.

RÂKIM: That is really surprising.

FELÂTUN: Wouldn't you like to meet her?

RÂKIM: If you don't mind . . . But are you willing to introduce this girl that you love so dearly to a stranger?

FELÂTUN: Oh, come on! You are talking like a rough Turk! Do we act that way in the *alafranga* lifestyle?

RÂKIM: Somehow I can't reconcile myself with the *alafranga* lifestyle . . .

While exchanging these words, they headed down to the crossroads to go to see the actress. It occurred to Râkım that this woman, who mourned so intensely for Felâtun's father's death, even going so far as to buy black mourning plates, must be a supremely skillful actress.

FELÂTUN: You are wandering again! You always go around lost in thought.

RÂKIM: It's nothing, my friend. There is just some work that I need to do.

FELÂTUN (*condescendingly*): Work, work, work! What is it with you and work? When are you ever going to be done with it, eh? You've earned enough money already! Live off what you have for a while.

RÂKIM: What can I do, my friend? I don't have any vineyards, farms, or rent income. What do we eat if we don't work?

FELÂTUN: You're not going to be young forever, for God's sake! After your beard turns grey, girls won't be interested in you anymore, even if you have money. One should enjoy one's youth! I guess you'll turn out to be just like my father. The poor man earned and saved, but couldn't even manage to eat in comfort. We should draw lessons from this, shouldn't we?

RÂKIM: May he rest in peace!

Râkım didn't comment on Felâtun Bey's erudite ideas. They walked in silence for a while.

RÂKIM: Did you hear the news, my friend? Somebody told me the other day that Reyhan Efendi has been appointed as the district governor somewhere in Anatolia. I was truly pleased to hear this.

FELÂTUN: Well, I hadn't heard the news! I haven't been to the government office since my father died. Sir, this strange girl is taking up all my time. She doesn't leave my side until the evening, and at night I absolutely have to *accompagner* her to the theater. So then what's the problem? Well, I have to wait for her and take her home afterwards. And when we get all the way back to her house, I can't just leave, you know . . . As a result I end up having to spend the night there. That's the problem!

RÂKIM: Trouble, but sweet trouble, no?

FELÂTUN: Do you even need to ask? She has the voice of a nightingale! The way she plays the piano is unparalleled. Especially that *éloquence*! She speaks so sweetly. And when she starts reading a poem from the works of well-known poets such as Racine, Boileau, and Molière . . . she sweeps people off their feet. I have never seen anyone read that way before. Even if you've never studied French, you'd still understand it. She even performs a *déclame* with her body to accompany her readings. She is obviously an actress! The thing that affects me the most is that she is so moved by her own reading: She cries and cries, and hugs me, embraces me and drowns me in her tears. I've never seen such a *sentimentale* woman!

Râkım knew that actresses could cry whenever they wanted to. While walking along and exchanging these words, they arrived at their destination, Hotel J——. That hotel wasn't for everyone but only for the purse-proud. After all, they charge five francs—in other words, twenty-five kuruş—for a coffee with milk. In fact, kuruş were not even used in that place! They walked into a private suite with a small living room and two bedrooms. The mademoiselle who Felâtun was crazy about came sashaying up to him with an attitude unique to sassy French women, gave him a hug, and kissed him.

FELÂTUN (*introducing Pauline to Râkım*): Je te présente mon . . . (Let me introduce my . . .)

PAULINE: Pas besoin, je ne suis pas une imbecile, on conçoit tout de suite que monsieur est un de tes amis. (No need, I am not an idiot, I can tell right away that this gentleman is a friend of yours.)

RÂKIM: J'ai l'honneur ma . . . (It's my honor, my . . .)

Although Râkım wanted to say something like "I pride myself in having the honor to meet you," in French, the woman didn't give him the chance and interrupted him.

PAULINE (*reciprocating Râkım's greeting*): Assez, Monsieur, assez. Ici, entre jeunes gens on ne fait pas ces bétises là. On y tutoit tout bonnement. (Enough, Monsieur, enough. Here, among young people we don't engage in that sort of nonsense. We use the familiar tu with one another quite comfortably.)

FELÂTUN (*to Râkım*): You see, my friend, how independent she is. Can one ever be bored with such a person? Sir, those *ceremonies* and *façons!*

RÂKIM: You're right, Sir, you're right! She *is* very pleasant!

The conversation after this point was held entirely in French.

PAULINE: Hey! Look at me Felâtun! You brought a friend here, aren't you going to offer him something?

FELÂTUN: Absolutely! Well spoken, Pauline. (Her name was Pauline.)

PAULINE: Perhaps some champagne?

RÂKIM: No, my friend! I am not a drinker. I'll have coffee.

PAULINE: What? How crude!

This conversation might seem strange to some readers but those who have travelled to the *alafranga* world know that we never exaggerate our descriptions. This is how coquettish French hussies talk. Especially theater whores!

RÂKIM (*responding to Pauline*): You're right, my friend. However, I don't lead the life of a *bon viveur*. I live off my own work and endeavors. Now, when I leave here, I will return back to my work.

PAULINE: This means you are an *ouvrier*, a manual laborer.

FELÂTUN: Yes! He lives off the labors of his pen.

PAULINE: Bravo! Are you a journalist, Sir?

RÂKIM: I write all sorts of things! I am a laborer who writes some small novels, plays, and some pieces for newspapers.

PAULINE: How wonderful! This means you are one of us. I mean, an artist.

FELÂTUN: He is also a poet!

RÂKIM: Not at all!

PAULINE: Of course he is. Quite so, but Sir, a few glasses of champagne would inspire the likes of you. (*To Felâtun*): And for us, masters of love, it would enflame our love. Isn't that so, monkey! Baboon! Rabbit!

FELÂTUN (*impudently*): My God, you're so right.

راقم ـ درد اما طانئل درد دكلی ؟
فلاطون ـ صورارمبدك یا ؟
سس بلبل ! بهانو امثالمز ! هله او
﴿ الوقائس ﴾ ادای کلام ! آغزندن
بالمر آغار . راسین بواو موليدر كی
شعرای بهاءك آنارندن بریسنی الله
آلورمی ؟ انسانی غشی ایدر . بن
بویله اوفو بشسده كورمدم كه ! هيچ
فرانسزجه بطامش اولسه ئبئه اكلارسك
قاری اسانبه اوقودغنی وجودبله
﴿ دقلامه ﴾ ادا وتفهم ايدبور .
نیازوجی بو ؟ معلوم آ ! كا الك زياده
تأثیرایدن شی قار بنك كندی اوقو بشدن
كندیسی دخی منأثر اولهرق هونكور
هونكور اغلامسی و اوحالسده بویله
صار یلوب وبی قوجافلابوب ـ كوز
باشلری ایچنده غرق ایندیر . بوقدرده
مسانئع انئالك حساس قاری كورمدم كه !
شو سوزری هم سو بلیدك هم
كیدرك واردجقاری بره دخی واردیلر .
لكن راقم برتبا زوبی قار بده اغلامق
ابسندد یكی زمان اغلایه بللك مهارتی دخی
اولدیغنی بلور ایدی . واردقاری بر
(ج) هونتی ایدی كه بوهوتلده هركس
بشابه میدرق اورابه كبدسنه كوونانلر
كیدبیلور . زیرا اورواده برسودل
قهوه بش فرانق يعنی یكرمی بش غروشدر

———

هله اوراده غروشك اسمی معلوم
دكادر آ ؟ كیده كیده بذاره محصوصه به
كربدبار كه بان باه ابكی اوطه رده كوچك
صالوندن عبارتدر . فلاطونی دیوانه
ایدن مادموازل فرانسز عشوه بازل بنه
محصوص اولان طور ایله صحرابهرق
كلدی بوشه صاردیه او بدی !

— je te présente mon...

[سكا تقديم ايدرم بنم ٠٠٠٠]

دیه فلاطون راقی تقديم ایتك ابستنه
مشیدی .

— pas besoin je ne suis pas
une imbecile, on conçoit tout de
suite que monsieur est un de tes
amis.

[زبجی یوق ! بناشك دكلم ؟ درحال
اكلاشبله بلور كه بواقندی سنك
دوستلركدن بریسیدر]

دیه مقابلهایدی . بونك اوزرینه
راقم

— j'ai l'honneur ma...

[افتخار ایدرم كه بنم ٠٠٠٠]

دیه الافرانكسدن اولدیغی اوزره
﴿ سرکلمه مشرف اولداهد افتخار
ایدرم ﴾ بولو برسوز سوله مك
ابسته مش ایدیسده قاری اكادنجی
میدان براقهرق :

RÂKIM: Can everyone state their opinion so freely?

PAULINE: Absolutely!

RÂKIM: In that case, I disagree. What use are poetic ideas roused by wine? What is the point of stimulating love and affection with wine?

PAULINE: *O là là!* Aha! So this gentleman is a philosopher! You should have been named Felâtun. (*To Felâtun*): Hey, you fat old cow! See, this gentleman isn't like you. You were going on about how all *you* need in this world is wine, music and a woman, right?

FELÂTUN: Loving you made me this way.

PAULINE: Just look at that yellow woodlouse! He is still stuck in his chair. Here, your guest has come. Now get up and . . .

FELÂTUN: Oh, yes! *Pardon.* They haven't fixed the rope of this servant bell, so now I have to go all the way to the apartment door and pull the big bell. (*He leaves.*)

PAULINE: Sir, I would like to tell you how happy I am to meet you. However, there is something not quite fitting. Writers are typically more independent. Yet, you seem even more bashful than I am.

RÂKIM: Isn't it good to be moderate in all things?

PAULINE: Our lobster Felâtun is such a saucy man. He has neither a helm nor a compass. He has lost his way, drifting in this ocean of love. You understand me, eh? I shouldn't care so much, but I love that rogue!

FELÂTUN (*back after giving the order*): I ordered a marvelous tea. I also asked for some rum, for those who want it.

PAULINE: You see now? This was probably the only time you've used your mind in your whole life. Those who want punch can drink punch, and those who want tea can drink tea.

They sat together and drank punch. While they chatted about this and that, Felâtun Bey prattled on about the incredible advantages of the *alafranga* lifestyle, and how such a lifestyle wouldn't be possible in the *alaturka* world. For instance, he said:

FELÂTUN: What are Turkish women good for? There is nothing like their arrogance and pride. With a little smile, she makes her lover come alive; then she hides the smile and pulls a long face. It's impossible to ingratiate yourself with a Turkish woman. Her coyness is unbearable, and her jokes are tasteless. You know it perfectly well, my friend, don't you? Let's say you purchased a female slave . . . What pleasure can liberal, independent, and free people like us get from a slave? Who knows whom she lost her heart to? As she's your slave, she's obliged to submit to you.

Râkım was taken aback when he heard Felâtun talk this way. Râkım wondered what wisdom there was in putting up with these French ladies when Ottoman ladies, despite their solemnity and pride, offered so many delights. If a man were to receive the kind of insults that Felâtun received from this lady, there was no question that he'd break that person's head. Râkım couldn't figure out why Felâtun put up with it. Especially when Felâtun brought up the subject of female slaves, Râkım almost burst into laughter. Yet again, he restrained himself and thought, "Silly you, doesn't a slave have feelings? It's a simple matter to buy a girl's freedom for five or ten kuruş. Just wait until you earn her love, then you'll see what a beloved she makes! Ah, my dear Janan! Poor little girl!" These thoughts ran through Râkım's mind but he didn't voice them out loud to Felâtun.

Finally, Râkım got up to go after spending more than an hour with this *alafranga* couple. He bid farewell to both, and Felâtun didn't neglect to see him off. When they arrived at the hotel's reception, Felâtun asked Râkım's opinion:

FELÂTUN: So what do you think?

RÂKIM: Great! (*smiling*) At least she doesn't spill mayonnaise sauce all over you!

FELÂTUN: Forget those English fools for God's sake! I am surprised that you are putting up with them for only four liras a month.

RÂKIM: What can I do, my friend? I need to earn a living.

FELÂTUN: Oh, for God's sake! This boy and his love for money . . . How about I give you four liras a month!

RÂKIM: Thank you, my friend. I'm content with what I have.

FELÂTUN: Don't take it the wrong way. I am telling you the truth. You think I can't afford to pay you four British liras a month?

RÂKIM: Not at all, my friend. Who said that? I'm just saying that I enjoy being with the Ziklas family.

FELÂTUN: What pleasure do you get from those carroty English girls? Man, you really don't know how to live. I mean, you could if you wanted to. In fact, you have one foot in Beyoğlu. Would it be so bad if you found a nice apartment and took a little mistress?

RÂKIM (*thinks of Josephine for a second, but doesn't utter a word about her since it would violate their secret*): That would be nice, but my friend, I can't see the benefit of that kind of wastefulness, for either of us.

FELÂTUN (*mockingly*): Wastefulness? Just a minute! You think I am that big of an idiot? If I were to calculate it, the money I earned these past three months might be equal to what I spent, if not more.

RÂKIM (*gladly*): Well then, if that's the case, then there's nothing for me to say. Life is good to the extent that it's prosperous. You can only live within your means. I trust that your sister lives comfortably. Because this is an important consideration too, don't you think?

FELÂTUN: Our philosopher Râkım prattling on about wisdom again. Go easy, brother. My earnings are in good order and the odds are in my favor.

RÂKIM: So tell me, what sorts of arrangements have you made? Commerce or something?

FELÂTUN: You know the kind of commerce men like us engage in.

RÂKIM: I don't know what you mean.

FELÂTUN: You know, in the evening you put forty or fifty liras in your pocket and head to the gambling parlor.

RÂKIM (*sullenly*): My!

FELÂTUN: Wait, not so fast. You start playing, and if the dice roll to your advantage, you win forty or fifty liras more and pull out.

RÂKIM: It's obvious you've only been playing for a month.

FELÂTUN: How did you know?

RÂKIM: Because leaving the game when one is losing or pulling out after winning just forty or fifty liras is a precaution taken only by novices. After a couple of months, as one gains more experience, this caution disappears.

FELÂTUN: Don't worry about me.

RÂKIM: I'm not worried about you. You won't be lost in gambling. I'm worried about a monthly income of fifteen or twenty thousand kuruş. You know very well that twenty or thirty thousand liras is a fortune that could easily be lost in gambling in the space of a few months.

FELÂTUN: So now you're going to start lecturing me on wisdom?

RÂKIM: No, *adieu* for now!

FELÂTUN: *Adieu, mon cher!*

Shall we tell you something surprising? After these two friends parted, they each went their own way thinking badly of each other. Felâtun thought, "Râkım doesn't have my fortune and he doesn't lead the life I do with such a mistress in a hotel like Hotel J. He is talking like this out of jealousy. If he also had 15,000 liras, then he'd admit that the way I live is perfectly normal and respectable." For his part, Râkım thought, "Since Felâtun was kicked out of the Ziklas household, now he wants to prevent me from going there by paying me four liras a month. How would I earn those four liras . . . can't I earn that by myself? Only sycophants rely on the unstable fortunes of such spendthrifts. Let that gentleman live as he likes. We've known a lot of people like him and learned from their experiences."

Whose opinion do you approve of? We approve of Râkım's. We know from experience that the fortune of a spendthrift, especially of one like Felâtun, is unstable.

There, these were all the incidents that took place before the arrival of spring; we described them, we're done.

Chapter 7

THE SPRING finally brought a sense of relief to the souls of the great and humble alike. The most important incident that deserves description is Râkım's outing in Kağıthane. It happened as follows:

Again, one lesson day, Râkım paid a visit to Josephine, with whom he still maintained a relationship, but only a sincere and friendly one. Their conversation that day concerned a Kağıthane outing. Josephine told Râkım that she had recently gone to Kağıthane with some women from a gentleman's household. Because they had gone on a Sunday, they found themselves stuck in their carriages, unable to actually see the fields that they had come to enjoy in the first place. Moreover, everyone else enjoyed the woman chasers who wandered around the carriages like thieves but Josephine couldn't bring herself to take pleasure in them.

RÂKIM: Kağıthane is truly one of the most beautiful places in the world, but you can't enjoy it on Fridays or Sundays. You have to do it the right way.

JOSEPHINE: What is the right way?

RÂKIM: Would you be willing to go?

JOSEPHINE: Would I be going by myself?

RÂKIM: Of course not! You'd be going with me.

JOSEPHINE (cheerfully): With you? Of course I would. I am sure we'd have a lot of fun.

RÂKIM: We could also take Janan. And my nanny, if you wanted.

JOSEPHINE: That sounds lovely.

RÂKIM: We could go either on a Tuesday or a Wednesday when those beautiful greens and meadows aren't crowded. We would truly enjoy what they have to offer. On other days, the place turns into a horse-and-carriage fair.

JOSEPHINE: Oh, we would have such fun.

RÂKIM: Also, when people go to Kağıthane, they bring along refreshments.

JOSEPHINE (*delightedly*): See, this is the true *alaturka* way of having fun. It makes even going out into the countryside a worthwhile experience.

RÂKIM: If you've agreed to come, let me know so that I can begin preparations.

JOSEPHINE: Just send me word the night before our outing, so I don't make other plans for the next day.

RÂKIM: Certainly.

After settling on this with Josephine and tutoring the English girls, he returned home in the evening.

Guess who welcomed him? Janan, of course. Râkım didn't mind her meeting him at the door anymore. It also pleased his nanny to see that Râkım didn't mind this. We already know full well that the way Janan expressed her position to Râkım when he mentioned a possible buyer had only heightened her joy and gaiety in his presence. If anyone were to witness how pure and sincere their heart-to-hearts were, one would take them for siblings.

As his nanny hadn't gone to sleep yet, the three of them sat together in the living room. Janan made some coffee and brought it to her master, to the master that she loved so dearly. As Râkım was sipping his coffee, he said:

RÂKIM: My dear Nanny! Why don't you go on an outing from time to time?

FEDAYI: We do, Sir!

RÂKIM: Oh come on, when was the last time you went anywhere?

FEDAYI: We go wherever Janan wants.

JANAN (*with an attitude indicating her special sympathy for Fedayi*): Dear Nanny takes me everywhere, Sir.

RÂKIM: Tell me where she takes you.

JANAN: To Salıpazarı.

RÂKIM: Salıpazarı is right outside our door.

FEDAYI: We even go to Tophane, Sir.

RÂKIM: No, no, my dear Nanny. I am talking about excursion spots like Ihlamur, for example.

FEDAYI: I took her there last summer. But Janan doesn't like those kinds of places.

RÂKIM: Maybe she'd like them now.

JANAN: Those are bad places, Sir. Men and women together! It's very bad! It makes me feel uncomfortable. I'd rather stay at home.

FEDAYI: I took her to Küçükçiftlik once. It wasn't a holiday, so it wasn't crowded and we enjoyed it.

JANAN: You're right, my dear Nanny! How we enjoyed that day! How wonderful the greenery was. Those trees, that pool. Oh, it was so beautiful!

RÂKIM (*feeling pleased at seeing the girl so happy*): See, that's good, so we should go again, right?

FEDAYI: We shall go once summer arrives. I wouldn't want my dear Janan to be uncomfortable.

RÂKIM: Of course not, my dear Nanny!

JANAN: Nanny loves me like her own daughter. And I love her like my own mother.

Having said that, she began hugging and kissing the loyal, compassionate, and gentle Fedayi.

RÂKIM (*feeling indescribably content at this scene*): No, you can't kiss Nanny like that in my presence. It is making me jealous.

With this, Râkım stood up and threw his arms around his nanny and kissed her. Poor Fedayi's eyes filled with tears as both Janan and Râkım hugged her:

FEDAYI (*referring to Râkım's mother*): Oh, my dear lady, the light of my eyes! Can you see this scene from up above?

RÂKIM (*with eyes filled with tears*): Here, my dear Nanny, you've taken the place of our mother. My mother's cheeks might have faded but yours are, thank God, hale and hearty.

The exchange caught Janan's attention as well. This affectionate scene didn't last long and all three of them sat back down. Afterwards,

RÂKIM: My dear Nanny! Would you take us to Kağıthane next Wednesday?

FEDAYI: You're coming too?

RÂKIM: Yes, I want to come.

JANAN (*leaping for joy*): Are you going to come with us, Sir?

RÂKIM: Indeed!

JANAN: All right, but there will be lots of people there, you won't be able to sit with us!

RÂKIM: There won't be anyone there on Wednesday. It will just be us.

JANAN (*feeling even happier*): Oh! Is that so? Please dear Nanny, will you take us?

FEDAYI: I will, I will, why wouldn't I?

RÂKIM: Even your teacher Josephine will join us.

JANAN (*with infinite happiness*): Is that so? Oh my God! Dear Nanny, Josephine is coming as well.

FEDAYI: Even better, we'll all be together.

RÂKIM: We will go early in the morning on Wednesday. I mean, very early!

FEDAYI: Will Josephine be able to come that early?

RÂKIM: Josephine will come here the night before and stay with us.

FEDAYI: Did you decide this together?

RÂKIM: No! I decided this on my own. We talked only about going to Kağıthane one day.

FEDAYI: Okay, Sir, but where is Josephine going to sleep?

RÂKIM: I've thought of that as well and made a decision. You will take me as a guest in your room for one night. Josephine will sleep in my room and Janan in hers.

FEDAYI: You know best, my son.

RÂKIM: No, my dear Nanny, *you* know best. Now, about the beds . . .

FEDAYI: What about them? We already resolved the sleeping arrangements.

How could we possibly describe Janan's happiness that night? She was happy that she was being treated like a daughter or a sister in the family. She was delighted about their upcoming trip to Kağıthane. And she was over-joyed about Josephine's accompanying them and spending a night at their house. Clearly, Janan loved Josephine as much as Josephine loved Janan.

After finishing his coffee and finalizing these decisions, Râkım retired to his room to do some writing. His nanny felt sleepy and went to bed. What about Janan? She didn't feel sleepy. She was out of her senses with happiness and didn't feel like reading. So she went and sat across from her master. While Râkım wrote, she prepared his cigarettes with the tobacco tin in front of her.

RÂKIM: Why aren't you going to sleep, Janan?

JANAN: I don't feel sleepy, Sir. If I am disturbing you, I shall go to my room and prepare your cigarettes there.

RÂKIM: You are not disturbing me. I never get enough of looking at you. I just wondered if you were comfortable.

JANAN (*fixing her looks up in the sky with gratitude*): What happiness!

Her attitude encouraged him to be forthcoming with his emotions, and he said:

RÂKIM: Janan!

JANAN: Yes, Sir?

RÂKIM: Never mind!

JANAN: You were about to say something, Sir, but, as you wish.

RÂKIM (*letting go of his pen*): I was just about to say . . . Janan!

JANAN: Yes, Sir?

RÂKIM: Do you know that I love you, my sweet Janan?

JANAN: How can I not know, Sir, of course I do! Didn't you tell me so yourself? Didn't you say, "I love you like a sister?"

RÂKIM (*standing up*): Ah, Janan, ah! But I don't love you like a sister. I love you like Janan.

JANAN (*a nice pink color spreading over her face and chest*): Am I not your property, Sir?

RÂKIM (*angrily*): Stop saying that! You are nobody's property! You own yourself. Ah, my dear Janan, for God's sake, don't you love me too? Tell me the truth!

Janan approached her master and they embraced each other.

JANAN: How shall I put this, Sir? You are talking as if you don't know how I feel.

RÂKIM: Ah, ah, Janan! *You* are talking as if you don't know how I feel. Say, "I love you," if you love me. Let me hear you say these words. These words would resurrect me. These would be the most delightful words in the whole world.

JANAN: I love you Sir, I honestly do. Ah, what else can I do but love you? How can I not love you? It's beyond my power not to love you.

More than Janan's uttering these words, her amorous delivery augmented Râkim's emotions. It was as if the insanity of the final stage of love appeared at the very beginning in his case. He said,

RÂKIM: Oh, my dear Janan, my dear Janan! In my heart, I honestly believe that you love me. I could listen to you repeat these words to me until morning.

Râkım's words moved Janan so much that she was about to melt. With her master already in her arms, she placed a passionate kiss on his eyes. Râkım nearly kissed her in return but timidly refrained:

RÂKIM: Janan, oh, Janan! I honestly feel jealous of myself. Oh God! Am I going insane or what?

It really came to the point where it wasn't possible to discern whether Râkım was going insane. So much so that Janan felt scared. She helped Râkım sit on the sofa and sat herself down beside him. For a while they sat in silence and kept looking into each other's faces. As their hearts were full to bursting, they almost couldn't breathe.

Felâtun's remarks about slaves crossed Râkım's mind; however, his mind wasn't strong enough to judge them, so he banished them from his mind, "Spare me, you fool! How could you know what is delightful in this world and how to enjoy it? You live like a slave with that flirtatious actress of yours!"

Râkım had been staring at Janan's face for a couple of hours when he drifted off to sleep on the sofa. Janan wanted to rise and go to her bed. However, as Râkım had just fallen asleep, she didn't have the heart to wake him up, and because the sofa was comfortable anyway, she remained there for a while, hungrily feasting her eyes on the face of her master, brother, lover, beloved, or whatever he was. Later, she rose and went to her bed with a heart filled with a thousand emotions.

The next morning, Râkım opened his eyes to find himself on the sofa and Janan sitting across from him. There was no change whatsoever in the girl's gravity and dignity! She was still the same Janan! Such gravity and dignity!

What were you thinking? We kindly request that you not assume Janan to be an importunate hussy. She is an honorable, polite, well-mannered, kind, and understanding girl through and through. When Râkım saw his nanny's smiling face, he realized that she knew about last night's romance. Yes, Nanny knew about it. However, don't think that Nanny was secretly watching or listening to them. No, esteemed readers, no! His nanny wasn't one to stoop to such ignominy. Janan shared it with her, for Nanny was her mother, confidante, and everything in this world. Janan always told her about everything that took place between her and Râkım, and received advice on how to behave in front of her master, which she followed to the letter. Who do you think the source of such fine manners and behavior, behavior that drove Râkım insane with love, was in the first place? His nanny raised this boy; she knew his morals and manners thoroughly. She instructed Janan in exactly the comportment that would make Râkım love her, even if he hadn't had feelings for her.

Râkım understood that his nanny knew about last night's incident but she didn't say a word to Râkım on that subject, so he didn't talk about it either. She only reminded him that it was Monday and if they were planning to go to Kağıthane on Wednesday, they had to start preparing; Râkım agreed and his nanny got to work.

Râkım was busy at work all day and kept himself occupied with some translating at home in the evening, so he managed to get through the night without finding himself completely caught up in the intense ardor of the night before.

Josephine was due to come the next evening, so after taking care of some business and making some preparations of his own, Râkım went to Beyoğlu later in the day to fetch Josephine. He found her at home since she only left her house on the days she gave piano lessons and stayed in when she didn't.

RÂKIM: *Bonjour*, my friend!

JOSEPHINE: *Bonjour*, Râkım!

RÂKIM: So, are you ready to go?

JOSEPHINE: Go where?

RÂKIM: To my place! Aren't we going to Kağıthane tomorrow?

JOSEPHINE: Oh, are we going to Kağıthane from your place?

RÂKIM: We'll spend the night at my place. You'll stay with us. We'll be on the sea very early tomorrow morning, even before sunrise. If we're going to do something, let's do it properly. Otherwise we'd miss out on the sunrise and the sunset. It's the right time of the year to see both of them.

JOSEPHINE: It sounds really good! But you don't have any place at your house for me to sleep, you crazy man!

RÂKIM: Don't worry about that, my dear. I arranged everything.

JOSEPHINE: All right, all right! You sit for a bit. I'll go get dressed.

Josephine stood up and went into another room to get dressed. Râkım sat and played around on the piano, and when Josephine finished dressing, they got going. They went down Posta Street to Postanebaşı, and by way of Tophane Avenue they gradually arrived in Salıpazarı. Janan saw Josephine as they entered the house and she ran to her with open arms. They kissed in greeting. Josephine also exchanged greetings with Nanny. Later Râkım, Josephine, and Janan settled in the living room. Nanny was busy getting things ready.

This evening was the first time Janan placed the rakı set on the sideboard in the living room. When Râkım offered Josephine the first glass, she again went on about how Istanbul's rakı was one of the most delightful drinks in the world and how she preferred it to wine. Then she picked up her glass and drank. Râkım joined Josephine as well. As they started drinking together, Janan settled herself in front of the piano and began playing the melodies that she knew best, masterfully. Râkım didn't get to see Janan playing the piano that often and was pleased with her talent. Moreover, he hadn't been able to discern how good her French had become while tutoring her; but tonight after listening to her conversation with Josephine he was impressed at her proficiency.

Listening to Janan play the piano made Josephine even happier and she went and joined her. Oh my God! Josephine's mastery of the piano was astonishing. You couldn't possibly imagine someone pressing eighty or a hundred piano keys with ten fingers all at once! But this is exactly what Josephine managed to do; it seemed as though she had four hands with ten fingers each.

Janan demonstrated her knowledge of cup-bearing impeccably, as if she had been serving as a cupbearer at drinking gatherings for forty years. She would keep filling Josephine's glass by the piano and performed the same service for her master. Her master would sip from the glass that he took from Janan's hands as if he were sipping fire.

Have you noticed how our drinking gatherings usually go? If you did, then you've probably realized that after some serious drinking, people always start showing and professing their love for each other. This happened at Râkım's gathering as well; however, the love between Râkım and Josephine was already confirmed, and Janan wasn't even remotely drunk, so it was Josephine who couldn't stop talking about how fond she was of Janan.

Finally it was time for dinner. The table was set in this same living room. After placing everything on the dinner table, they all sat down to eat. Although Nanny felt very content about seeing such a gathering in the house, she was a bit bothered by the presence of alcohol. But would she let her dear Râkım, her son and master, know about her discontent? Nanny had already prepared feasts at larger events and the food she cooked received particular attention from Josephine. They ate and drank with great appetite. They remained seated, and Janan served coffee at the dinner table. After an hour or so of eating fruits and chatting about this and that, Josephine eventually retired to sleep in Râkım's bed, which had been prepared for her, and Râkım went to sleep in the bed that had been laid out in his nanny's room.

Of course, Janan went to her room.

But wait, we can't confirm that yet.

Hold on, what happened?

Here is what happened:

Isn't it clear that Janan would remain with Josephine until she had helped her undress and get into bed? How could someone in Josephine's condition—in other words, as a woman who was able to disregard her past adventure with Râkım and loved Janan dearly, not ask Janan a thousand questions? Accordingly, while she got undressed, she asked Janan:

JOSEPHINE: Janan, my dear!

JANAN: Madame!

JOSEPHINE: You help your master undress like this, don't you?

JANAN: My master? Yes, of course I do.

JOSEPHINE: Does he at least behave himself while undressing?

JANAN: Oh! Why shouldn't he? Is he a child?

JOSEPHINE: Men are worse than children. When children are undressing, they stamp and sweat. Children with moustaches, on the other hand, hug your neck.

JANAN (*embarrassed*): For goodness sake, Madame! Listen to what you are saying!

JOSEPHINE: What am I saying? Am I saying something inappropriate?

JANAN: It is inappropriate indeed!

JOSEPHINE: Oh, then it surely means that he doesn't behave himself while undressing. If he did, you wouldn't find anything inappropriate in this conversation.

JANAN: My dear mistress, don't say such words to me.

JOSEPHINE: Oh, you crazy girl! What are you embarrassed about? Isn't he your master? What's so wrong it? You're both young and beautiful. It'd be more inappropriate if he behaved himself while undressing.

JANAN: Not at all! Our master is very well behaved and modest.

JOSEPHINE: Come on, tell me, do you think you can you fool me? You are acting as if I don't know. Oh, my dear child! Your master told me all about it. He never keeps any secrets from me. How much you both cried the other night.

Janan was on the verge of believing these words and revealing her secret to Josephine. However, since she wasn't familiar with the adventures between her master and Josephine and suspected that Josephine might be trying to sound her out, she resolved to keep her secret since she thought it dishonorable to reveal her encounters with her master to somebody other than Nanny. Yes, this is how reserved our Janan was. She said:

JANAN: Master loves me like his sister. He never teases me. He told you whatever he told you. How can I know what he said?

JOSEPHINE: Oh, my dear Janan. Here is a lover trying hard to keep her feelings to herself! It's all right, my dear, it's all right! Young people like you who don't know the rules of love always act this way. I'd like to congratulate both of you. Honestly, you deserve each other. May God bless you and keep you together. Do you understand me, my dear? Râkım is a sentimental man. You should handle him well. If you handle him well, you can easily get him to commit himself to you.

Now, after this interrogation, they chatted a while longer, then Josephine got into bed and dismissed Janan. But in what state did she leave the girl? Janan was wide awake with all the emotions of a couple nights ago racing through her heart.

There came a "knock, knock" on the front door sometime early the next morning while everyone was still asleep. Nanny woke up first, and then woke Râkım. It turned out to be the rower, Old Osman. They looked at the time; it was around five. Râkım said, "All right, it's time, we should start getting ready," and he went downstairs with his nanny to give Old Osman the equipment that was to be placed on the boat. Afterwards, he went to wake Janan.

Oh, how this thing called love makes people feel revitalized! After watching Janan, who was lying sprawled on the bed, for quite some time, he put his right hand on the girl's heart and then made a little sound. He noticed how her heart woke up even before she did. Have you ever noticed this? We certainly have. And we know how sweet it is. The heart that beats so softly and steadily while one sleeps starts beating with excitement when one wakes up. Especially if it is the heart of a lover like Janan! Try it and see for yourself!

Janan was startled when she woke up in the dark and saw her master standing in the faint light of the weakly lit oil lamp. She managed to say, "What happened, Sir, what can I do for you?" Râkım said, "Did you forget? We are going to Kağıthane. Come on, wake up. Light the fire and get ready. Wake Josephine up so we can enjoy the morning together. In the meantime we can arrange things." Janan jumped out of bed and got to her feet.

Why should we lie? It's surely better to tell the truth. It's not anything inappropriate anyway. The poor girl hugged her master's neck while getting out of bed. If you wish, you can regard this as impertinence. Her master excused her.

Everyone was up within half an hour. As the fire hadn't burned itself out yet, Janan brought a huge brazier into the living room, which cheered everyone up.

A coffee pot was set on one side of the fire, a teapot on another, and a pot containing freshly delivered cow's milk on yet another. The coals burned.

Josephine, in line with *alafranga* custom, wouldn't normally appear in front of a man in her nightclothes. However, she saw Râkım in the living room in his nightclothes with only a thin, fur coat thrown over his shoulders and he told her not to worry about formalities and to come join them. Hence they all sat groggily in their nightclothes. Coffee was made. They decided to start by drinking coffee, and then for their second cup people chose between coffee or tea with or without milk, according to their own tastes.

JOSEPHINE (*enjoying this Ottoman morning pleasure*): This is really marvelous!

RÂKIM: What is?

JOSEPHINE: Waking up early in the morning and seizing these pleasures.

RÂKIM: Do you like it, Madame?

JOSEPHINE: I really do, I can easily say that I've never woken up before sunrise in my life. How nice! Now we know that in an hour the sun will appear and we'll get to see it. Isn't that right?

RÂKIM: What's more, we'll see the sunrise on the water.

JOSEPHINE: Won't we be chilly?

RÂKIM: We have fur coats, woolen blankets, shawls, and coats. We won't be chilly. Especially since we'll have rum.

JOSEPHINE: I am really enjoying this. Râkım, can I tell you the truth? Everything about the Turks is better than the Europeans.

RÂKIM: No, Madame, not quite! Well, yes, we do enjoy winter mornings this way . . . however, can you deny that Europe also offers many entertainments?

JOSEPHINE: I am not lying, Râkım. I really mean it. Well, Europe does have many entertainments but they are *monotone* and always regulated. For one thing, when winter nights are long, people don't go to sleep before twelve o'clock in *alafranga* time, I mean, midnight. People even stay up until two sometimes! Thus, when we wake up we see that morning has already arrived. What I'm trying to say is that we only enjoy nighttime and deprive ourselves of sunrise, when nature awakes from her sleep.

RÂKIM: That's true.

JOSEPHINE: I wouldn't say it if I wasn't sure. I know what I'm talking about. For one thing, you can't find this Turkish hospitality in Europe. I'm not saying that they don't visit each other's homes. Yet, their balls and dinners are always formal affairs. Everyone spends time with their own family when they go to someone else's place. It's very unusual for someone to spend time with another family.

As Josephine liked taking full advantage of the world, she paid particular attention to those things that sweeten our existence. She proved her point regarding Europe's disagreeable aspects but couldn't find such disadvantages in the way Ottomans lived. This little get-together lasted for more than half an hour.

Since they had decided to be on the water before sunrise, everyone got up to get dressed. It was the last days of March and sunrise was around six, so they dressed quickly and hurried to the port.

Old Osman's new boat had two pairs of oars and was wide and beautiful. Râkım had Josephine and his nanny sit in the back, while he sat in the front with his Janan. Since everyone was wearing a fur coat and had a woolen blanket stretched over their legs, there was no need to complain about the morning chill.

They pushed off the Salıpazarı pier. As they put out to sea, the day was newly breaking over Üskudar. Rowing slowly, they had already passed the two bridges and found themselves at the Bay of Tersane as the first light of day was shooting from the horizon into the vastness of the sky. Full light of day caught this happy and joyful party as they neared Sütlüce.

Oh, what a splendid morning it was! Oh, how happy this splendor made Josephine feel! And Janan, how it made Janan feel! Râkım continued to respond tenderly to the hundreds of questions that Janan had continuously been asking since leaving Salıpazarı, and to her and everyone else's delight, he peppered his answers with terms of endearment like, "My dear!" "Honey!" and "Sweetheart!"

JOSEPHINE: Râkım, you have such a good nature! You are humane, fortunate and happy!

RÂKIM: Thank God, I am fortunate and happy. Yet I don't consider my humanity to deserve such praise.

JOSEPHINE: Your humanity is enhanced by your happiness. Your good nature allows for such happiness.

RÂKIM: More compliments! But what's the reason?

JOSEPHINE: The reason is this: I can attest that this delightful trip couldn't happen anywhere in Europe. Even one in a hundred residents of Istanbul wouldn't have thought of arranging a trip like this.

RÂKIM: Very true. Yet I don't think we deserve such praise for this. The morning, the sea, and this beautiful place . . . these are all God's creations. We owe
our boat to the civilizational progress of mankind. These are all blessings
that one should appreciate. Let's concentrate on our journey now. God has
given me an intimate companion like you, a friend like Janan and a mother
like Nanny. In addition to all of these blessings, He gave me the strength to
earn enough in two hours to provide for this delight, this journey, and these
amusements. It would be a shame if I didn't enjoy these blessings to the full-
est now that I've been offered them.

JOSEPHINE: I congratulate you for this achievement! And especially the way you
reason! Râkım, God knows, I'd stand up and kiss you on your mouth if I
weren't ashamed to do so in front of everyone else.

When she heard what Josephine said, Janan immediately glanced
at her face, though she quickly collected herself and didn't reveal her
thoughts. Nevertheless, after hearing her master's reasoning, her love for
him grew to the point where she snuggled against Râkım and got into his
arms. As a result, the boat became unbalanced, so Old Osman said, "Little
lady, little lady! Can you please recline a little?" and Janan regained her
equilibrium.

Just as the morning breeze brought the musky smell of the surroundings to our ensemble, they arrived at Çoban Çeşmesi. Can you guess what
crossed Râkım's mind? Let's see. He told Josephine,

RÂKIM: Hey, listen! The lady who has never taken a morning trip, who hasn't
tasted the pleasures of Istanbul! Do you know what just occurred to me?

JOSEPHINE: It must be something good.

RÂKIM: I think it's good; I'm not sure what you'll think.

JOSEPHINE: Come on, tell me, what is it?

RÂKIM: I have a craving for fresh sheep's milk. Would you like some?

JOSEPHINE: Is that even possible?

RÂKIM: Why shouldn't it be possible? Do you also have a craving for it? Just tell
me!

JOSEPHINE: Sure, why not?

RÂKIM (*to the rower*): Old Osman, do you know what just crossed my mind?

OLD OSMAN: What, Sir?

RÂKIM: I was wondering if we could find a dairy around here and drink some fresh milk. I mean further down, near the Alibey Stream, but any place will do.

You probably think that this request was bothersome for the rowers! To be honest, it really was bothersome to turn back after having come all the way to Çoban Çeşmesi. But not for Old Osman. Because he was Râkım's neighbor and knew this young man well. So, without any hesitation, Old Osman said,

OLD OSMAN: Very well, Sir, why not? We're already in the boat. Our arms aren't tired yet. We can keep wandering and if we get bored, we'll go to Eyüp Sultan.

RÂKIM: Bravo, Old Osman!

OLD OSMAN: Just because you see some grey in his beard, do you think that Old Osman has become an old man? If I start rowing from here, I'll get to Beykoz in no time at all.

RÂKIM: May God give strength to your arms, Old Osman!

While saying these words, Old Osman began to pull back the right oars and push the left ones and turned the boat around. They found a dairy at the mouth of the Alibeyköy stream and the flock of sheep was still there, having just been milked. Janan and Josephine gazed at the sheep and lambs from afar with pleasure. Râkım called the dairyman over and had him bring a couple bowls of fresh milk. They drank it thirstily. We should also mention that each rower drank as much as two or three men would have.

After this, they pushed off, passed Çoban Çeşmesi, and this time put ashore near the waterfalls. They put their things ashore and spread their blanket under a tree.

Now, we can cut the rest of this story of the Kağıthane outing short by saying, "They enjoyed themselves greatly and then returned home." However, is there any need for that? If we were to cut everything short, we could've told this story in a single page rather than in an entire volume. Besides, those who go to Kağıthane for an entire day don't just sit there the entire time. As Old Osman was accustomed to drinking coffee, he quickly rustled up a fire. Coffee was set on the fire, heated, and drunk. Later, Râkım and Josephine took Janan along and began wandering around under the trees near the water and up into the meadows. Poor Janan, isn't she still a child after all? When she saw herself in this meadow, as wide as a poet's imagination, her enthusiasm and merriment grew just as wide and she leapt and ran about ardently. She came up with excuses for her playfulness, and Josephine understood:

JOSEPHINE: Janan, can you catch me?

JANAN (*rejoiced*): Of course I can.

RÂKIM (*realizing what was going on*): No, you can't catch her. Go on then, run!

Josephine began to run. Janan ran after her. With zigzags and twists, Josephine made the girl run pretty well. So much so that they both turned red and were out of breath. Later, when they came back and reunited with Râkım, Josephine said slowly, "I entertained the child but now I'm exhausted!"

This trip to the meadows lasted for nearly an hour. Then they returned to their original spot. It was already a couple hours after sunrise. They were famished, as they had woken up early that day, so they had some breakfast. During breakfast they continued to talk about the beauty of Kağıthane and how splendid it was to watch the sunrise on the sea. Later on, they listened to Janan express her delight.

There was almost no one at Kağıthane that day. Even by midmorning, only an Armenian family had settled in the upper meadows. Josephine voiced her regret at not having remembered to bring her guitar along. She sang a few songs but without a guitar the audience didn't take as much pleasure in it. If one were to make a proper effort to contemplate the surroundings of such a strikingly beautiful place, one could surely find enough beauty in nature to ponder until nightfall, or even an entire week. Yet, it's human nature to keep looking for additional entertainment, which our people did. Their first entertainment was to resettle themselves on the other side of the tree away from the sun, which had invaded their location and was becoming bothersome. At Nanny's suggestion, each of them gripped one side of their blanket and carried it into the shade. Their next entertainment was to have Janan memorize the lyrics to some French songs. What a smart girl! She would learn a song of fifteen to twenty couplets in as many minutes, and she would never forget it.

This entertainment lasted for another hour or so, and then they set down to eat their late morning meal. At Râkım's suggestion and with Josephine's consent, they drank two glasses of *rakı*. Later, they took out the cold meat, stuffed grape leaves, halva, and grilled beef patties, which had been prepared by Nanny, and set aside shares for the rowers. They ate joyfully for about an hour. During this time, another boat passed by and a group of people disembarked near the waterfalls and walked up to the center of the meadows, where they settled.

After the meal, sleep, which had begun to overwhelm them in the growing warmth of the day, finally got the better of them. With the exception of Nanny, the three others moved to the shady side of the tree and lay down on the blanket and slept. Oh, dear Nanny! Was there any greater pleasure in this world than seeing Râkım Efendi having fun? She was enlivened by the delight these youngsters were taking in that day.

It was late afternoon when they woke up from their nap. They made another trip up into the meadows while Nanny placed their things on the boat. When they returned an hour later, the boat was ready to depart.

They got onto the boat. After rowing slowly for half an hour, they arrived at Azapkapısı and dropped Josephine off. Although Râkım requested that she stay with them again that night, Josephine excused herself, saying that she had work to do the next day. The rest of the group went to the Tophane waterfront, where they watched all the mosques in Üsküdar drowning in the golden light of the last rays of the sun. Still watching this beautiful sight, they reached their house fifteen minutes after the evening call to prayer.

Chapter 8

DID YOU ENJOY hearing about Râkım's outing to Kağıthane? Don't think our question silly. Not many people enjoy these sorts of outings. If you've ever examined the particular conditions of human beings, you would agree with us. The human condition dictates that a person cannot be satisfied if he's the only one to know about his happiness. He wants to let everybody else know about it. In fact, even when a person isn't actually happy, he resorts to trickery and deception to make others believe that he is happy. This human need is so common that we don't notice it. Yet, a common example of this need is showing off by paying twenty-five liras or more for diamonds to adorn a watch chain that only cost five liras in the first place. All right then, let us consider this:

It's true that people need watches. But what is the function of the chain? Since all it does is hold the watch, a simple cord would do. Well, no, it's not quite like that. People want the entire world to see what a great fortune they have, and that even the cord used to hold the watch is worth twenty-five gold coins. But what is the purpose of such showing off?

We already told you. It gives pleasure! Now, there are different degrees of duplicity, this one being the lowest all the way up to where people deem it necessary to come up with all sorts of meaningless lies to go around like Croesus. Let's look at this from another angle: The purpose of going on public outings isn't simply to enjoy the countryside, wilderness, fields, meadows, and flowers, but rather to see the public—or, more precisely—to show off in public. Isn't this, in a way, dictated by human nature? It's for this reason that we find at least twenty thousand people at excursion spots. If one were to think thoroughly about the kind of pleasure that one derives from suffocating in the dust and dirt of five, six hundred, or maybe even a thousand carriages—instead of sitting under a tree—and from presenting himself to those who are only ten steps away, he'd come to hate these excursion spots. However, the habitués of these outings don't think this way. When they go to excursion spots, they don't think about the beauty of the location and when they converse about the excursion, they don't mention it. They are only concerned with whether there is a crowd or not. When they like an excursion spot, they display their enthusiasm by saying, "Good heavens, one should have seen Kağıthane the other day. What a crowd, my God! Everybody, everybody! Was there anyone who wasn't there, anyone?"

Knowing that's how it generally is, we asked whether or not the readers enjoyed hearing about Râkım's Kağıthane outing. If not, then would you enjoy hearing about another Kağıthane outing?

It was a Friday, and in fact, one of those Fridays when Kağıthane was really crowded. And on that day in the meadows of Kağıthane, the bright gazes of a couple thousand eyes were all fixed on one spot.

What was there on that spot?

A perfectly adorned two-horse carriage. In it was a perfectly adorned madame. But the reader needs to pay attention when we say, "perfectly adorned." She wasn't adorned the way other madames typically are. Such ornaments as diamonds and pearls are observed on other madames only rarely. This madame was drowning in diamonds and pearls. In front of the carriage were two bands, one playing classical and the other popular instruments. Each of these bands was made up of two or three teams and each of these teams was composed of fifteen or twenty people.

To one side of this spectacle, five or six gentlemen were sitting on stools. Ice cream, cookies, and whatnot arrived on numerous trays and made their first stop at the carriage. After offering the wares to the carriage, the sellers would then serve the gentlemen. If the bands were playing *alaturka* tunes, then the gentlemen would request the songs, and if they were playing *alafranga* tunes, then the people in the carriage would be the ones to request them. If the tunes requested were performed as desired, then one lira would come flying into the air and fall in the middle of the musicians; the glances of those close by would move in an arch in conformity with the curving motion of the coin in the air.

In return for the giggles radiating their sparkle from the carriage, sighs from the gentlemen's side would fly about, and in this way, reputation and fame were dropped onto the stage of this world. This situation continued for one and a half to two hours, and then the madame ordered her carriage to move along. A very handsome, young, and fashionable man on a beautiful horse set off after it. All glances remained on them until they'd gone quite a distance, when the remaining gentlemen said, "Well done, this fellow is throwing money away hand over fist but he is certainly entertaining himself like a prince!"

How about that? Did this outing conform to our readers' expectations? See, the "prince" we've just described was our very own Felâtun Bey. Shall we tell you about how this outing came about?

One night, Felâtun Bey's throw of the dice somehow didn't serve him well in the game. But this hadn't been the case for the last fifteen days. Maybe he would have taken a break from the game for a few days if his lover, Mademoiselle Pauline, hadn't compelled him to play. Mademoiselle Pauline insisted on appearing in the casino and—as she put it herself—wanted to show off how proud she was to be Felâtun Bey's mistress. Because of her insistence, Felâtun Bey found himself obliged to continue playing. On that night when his dice didn't serve him well, and they really didn't, Pauline still insisted that he not hold back from putting a handful of gold coins on the table.

In short, that night he incurred a loss of about 700 liras. The pain of this loss clearly ate at his heart, and when they arrived back in their private room, Felâtun pulled a long face. He even suggested that Pauline was to blame for his loss.

PAULINE: Just look at this monkey! You annoying baboon! It's fine when you win but now that you lose, it's somehow my fault?

FELÂTUN: Fine my dear, but now I've lost 2,000 liras in the past week.

PAULINE: Look at this avaricious, greedy creature! The money you lost didn't go into my pockets, did it? What would you do if you were gambling in the famous German resort of Baden-Baden? Loss and gain go together. You lose one day, you win the next.

FELÂTUN: I am not saying that I can't win. But you're the one who ruins my concentration. You should leave me to my own devices. I know how the game works.

PAULINE (*enraged*): Oh, really? So, now I am misleading you! All right then, all right! From now on, such a deceptive woman as I shall not mislead you. Find another partner for yourself, Sir. And I shall find one for myself, a partner whom I won't mislead.

After saying these words, the woman turned her head toward the window. Felâtun, who came close to going mad with love for her, regretted what he had done, fell on his knees, and begged for her forgiveness. Although he confessed to being mistaken and at fault, as well as impudent, impertinent, and asinine, he couldn't win Her Majesty Mademoiselle Pauline's mercy and compassion.

How strange! Enough is enough, eh?

Well, this is how the game is played in the *alafranga* world. If you aren't familiar with it, let us inform you:

Esteemed readers, when an *alafranga* man burns with love for a European girl, and when she sees that she has thoroughly hooked him, she adds a dash of resentment to the relationship. This is how she inflames his love and as a consequence ensures that she gets what she wants. Mademoiselle Pauline had gotten Felâtun to this point, and even if the issue of losing money gambling hadn't come up, she would have created another opportunity to stir up conflict.

What if she couldn't create one? What would she do then?

You are asking too many questions! If there were no reason, is it so difficult to make something up? Can't one simply cause resentment by declaring, "I hear that you love another woman. I should have known. Go live with her from now on. Leave me alone!" We know an *alafranga* gentleman who wasn't only abandoned on a similar pretext but even got slapped!

Poor Felâtun! After realizing that it wasn't possible to conciliate the woman, he went out of the room with his head lowered in humility, rented another room, and spent the night there. The next day, although he went to her room to beg for forgiveness again, Pauline refused to admit him, and he returned in even greater despair and weariness. For an instant, the appropriate course of action crossed his mind and he thought, "Why, why do I keep begging this slut? Isn't this my own money? I pleased this wicked woman, drowned her in diamonds but I can't seem to ingratiate myself with her. There are a thousand other women just like her." However, his thoughts immediately shifted. "But oh, where else can I find those eyes? That beauty, those jokes, that coquetry! I can't bear this! I will do whatever I can; I must succeed! And . . . what will people say if they hear? I would be disgraced in front of my friends and enemies!" These thoughts threw him for a loop and on the second day of their fight, he succeeded in making up with her by begging her like a dog, throwing himself at her feet and agreeing to buy her a fair amount of diamonds.

So there! Now you know how the Kağıthane outing came about. It was Felâtun's expression of gratitude to Pauline for having reconciled with her.

Do you recall Mihriban? Mihriban ended up getting married! What? She's married? After her father's death, when Felâtun Bey stopped showing up at his father's house, the neighbors began giving her advice, and she married a thirty-year-old level-headed and educated captain who'd been all over the place. At first her husband found the poor girl flighty and didn't like her much; however, after recognizing her potential to become cultured, he thought that abandoning her wouldn't be as chivalrous as trying to educate her. Hence, he offered the girl much fatherly advice, brotherly suggestions, husbandly warnings, and cured her of her flightiness, thus making her love him as a loyal friend. Now Mihriban lives like a proper lady possessing a whole fortune made up of her husband's money and her own inheritance.

Yes! It's different with women. Flighty wives can often pull themselves together if they accept the discipline offered by their sensible husbands. The problem is that flighty men usually can't accept advice given by sensible wives and end up making their wives miserable.

Now compare this to Felâtun Bey's situation. Felâtun Bey, in addition to his utter flightiness, fell into Pauline's hands. She was the type to benefit from his destruction. But do you think that the advice of a loyal friend would make any difference? Not a chance! How many young men like him, men who devoured the fortune they inherited from their fathers, do we need to show you? Do you know how much advice was given to each of them? Did any of it make a difference? To the contrary, it only served to increase their profligacy.

No need for other examples. Felâtun Bey received his share of advice. When Râkım learned about Felâtun's adventure with Pauline in Kağıthane, he thought, "There! It's turning out as I predicted! He has taken pleasure from insulting me over and over. However, if I get stuck on such inconsequential matters, I might consent to the destruction of an acquaintance. And that would be contemptible. I should go and warn him." Accordingly, one day he found Felâtun and talked with him in person. "My friend! I couldn't bring myself to keep you from pleasure and joy. I am not in a position to give you advice. You know the far corners of this *alafranga* world better than I do. You've read so many French novels. Have you ever read about someone who was enlightened after forming a romantic attachment to a theater actress? It isn't necessary for these stories to have taken place in real life. Writers always talk about possibilities. One should enjoy reading them but also take lessons from them. Is it possible for a foreign slut to make a lover of you?" Although Râkım spoke in a friendly and decent way, and said everything he could think of, Felâtun still somehow didn't believe that these words were coming from a loyal friend. He thought, "Râkım is certainly jealous of my well-being," and didn't take any of Râkım's advice to heart. Moreover, he countered Râkım's arguments with his own evidence and refuted Râkım's fatherly advice bit by bit. Supposedly, Pauline had abandoned her career in the theater for him! She had given up her nightly income of thirty or forty liras solely out of love for Felâtun. And apparently Râkım didn't know every nook and cranny of the world of love and affection! What pleasure could one derive in this world if one lived like a piece of wood anyway? One isn't young forever! And so on, and so forth . . .

This is how people are. Especially the young ones. They insist on experiencing everything for themselves and refuse to be guided by others' experiences. So they learn life's lessons the hard way.

Our lives are so short that we can't experience all of life's lessons first-hand. If we recognize and learn from other's experiences, then maybe we can manage to live more comfortably, freely, and honorably.

Anyhow, we're not here to give the esteemed readers lessons in wisdom, are we? Let's attend to the delights of our story: It's been quite some time since we last heard about the Ziklas family.

It goes without saying that Râkım continued going to the English household to fulfill his duty of teaching the girls twice a week. Râkım, whose poetic and amorous sensibilities were heightened by Janan's love, never felt like leaving the Ziklas household, where he experienced an indescribable symphony from the way the girls spoke their now very competent Turkish in their own unique accent and intonation. Likewise, Mr. and Mrs. Ziklas appreciated Râkım more and more every day. But at the same time, it came to the point where the girls almost stopped going out of their house for they couldn't enjoy entertainments like balls and the theater anymore. If their parents were invited to some gathering, they would make their apologies and not attend. When people inquired about Jan and Margaret at the gatherings, their parents would say, "They are solely occupied with their teacher. If you give them a Turkish or Persian book, they won't even want to eat or drink." There were more people who understood this situation and appreciated it than those who couldn't. Once, a person belonging to the latter group asked Mr. Ziklas:

— My dear friend, are you going to convert these girls to Islam?

MR. ZIKLAS: No!

— Then, what's the purpose of forcing them to study this much Turkish?

MR. ZIKLAS: Nobody is forcing them. They are compelling themselves to do it.

— Fine. But it has come to the point where these girls no longer appear at any gatherings. If you were going to marry them to a Persian or a Turk tomorrow, then I'd understand . . .

MR. ZIKLAS: To be honest, I'll tell you this. I hope that our girls don't end up spinsters like Catholic nuns.

— You see what I mean!

MR. ZIKLAS: But it's fine, they're still young. They have a few cousins on their uncle's side and some cousins on their aunt's side of the family; surely the girls will marry one of them. Some of them are in India, some in Arabia; in short, they are all in eastern countries. They'll be pleased to know that the girls are learning Turkish.

— I'm also concerned about two young girls being left alone at home with a young teacher while you are at such gatherings.

MR. ZIKLAS: No, see, I can't entertain such concerns. God knows, Râkım Efendi is better mannered than our girls. And I'm not the only one who thinks that. All of Beyoğlu trusts him.

Our purpose in recounting these conversations is to show you the degree to which the Ziklas family loved and trusted Râkım more and more every day. Especially the girls. They didn't think about anyone but Râkım and were never without their Turkish books.

Ever since he'd first introduced the girls to one of Hafez's poems, they begged him to recite a couple more from his collected works at the end of each session, and they copied their favorite couplets along with their translations into their journals. Finally, at their request, Râkım promised to teach them Hafez's collected works from beginning to end. We want to explain to you the way he carried out this promise but since our intention is not to quote the entirety of Hafez's collected works here, we'll only show the esteemed readers how they read Hafez for the first time. If we show this, and if the esteemed readers pay attention to which couplets the girls chose to study and how Râkım paraphrased those couplets, then my readers will derive a very clear understanding of their relationship. It went as follows:

When Râkım read the first poem that begins with "You there, O Saqi (cupbearer) / fill a goblet and send it around," and paraphrased it, the girls didn't find a single couplet worth recording in their notebooks. As they didn't have a grain of mysticism in their nature, their minds were unable to access the delights of the spiritual world. They continued with the second poem that started with: "When will this desire be realized / o Lord, that they ally/ Our mind, all composed, and your disheveled hair," Râkım paraphrased it as: "My soul longs to see you adorned in beauty / with disheveled locks of curly hair/ But, what is the use? / Whenever your curls are disheveled, so is my mind / Oh God, when will this desire suffice and give way to the sudden unification of the entirety of my soul with your scattered curls?" Jan and Margaret quickly took up their pens and began recording this couplet with its translation. Afterwards, they eagerly noted down the following couplet and its translation:

> The soul that is at the end of its rope plans to see you. Shall it hold out
> or shall it let go. What is your command?

Râkım paraphrased this couplet as: "I melted with the sorrow of your love. I have no hope left for what remains of my life. Now my sweet life has risen to my lips and longs to see you. Should it spring forth and leave or should it return to its place, what is your command?"

The girls responded to this couplet with such enthusiasm that they almost erased the previous one from their notebooks. Yet, the next couplet amazed them even more, and they recorded it with complete astonishment. Here it is with its translation:

> Keep your skirt far from the dust and blood when you pass by us.
> For there are many slain in this path, sacrificed to you?

"The beauty of your face, the intensity of your perfection created disarray in this world. Everyone considers themselves blessed to be your sacrifice. To see the lovers' condition, as you walk through our neighborhood, lift your skirt to keep it from the blood, soil, or rather from this dreadful mud kneaded with blood, for there have been many to shed their blood and to sacrifice themselves for you, your victims."

They didn't select any other couplets from this poem. They also didn't choose any couplets from the poems starting with, "Saqi, brighten our chalice with the light of wine," "Sufi, come, for the chalice is poor mirror," and "Saqi! Arise and fill up the chalice." They found that the poem starting with "I'm losing the handle of my heart, you who have a heart, for God's sake (help)!" was incomprehensible, and although they found a couple of noteworthy poetic descriptions in the poem, "The garden again has the splendor of youth," they decided not to copy them down as they didn't enjoy them as much as the others. When they read the poem starting with, "If that Shirazi Turk would satisfy my heart," they found the following couplet very rich and colorful:

You spoke ill of me, and I am content. God forgive you, you spoke well!
A bitter answer befits ruby sugar-shedding lips.

Râkım paraphrased this couplet elegantly as follows: "The disarray caused by my passionate desire for you rendered me unconscious and stole my sanity. As a result, I commit thousands of impertinences with everything I say and do. Finally, you resented the disarray of my language and spurned me disdainfully. You scolded me. A scolding I enjoyed. Would such bitter words suit those ruby-lips, that sugar-eating and sugar-spilling mouth? Surely, any word tastes sweet, coming out of that rose-mouth."

Afterwards, they read the poems starting with "Morning breeze, gently tell that lissome gazelle," and "Last night from the mosque our master came to the wine tavern," but couldn't find anything worth recording in them. The poems starting with "To the retainers of the sultan who will convey this salutation" and "Where is the right thing to do and where am I in my ruined state" were received similarly. Only this following couplet from the poem "We've gone, you and our sorrowing heart know (why)" was selected:

If all the horizons gather around your head.
It is not possible that desire for you be driven from my head.

Râkım paraphrased this daring couplet audaciously as follows: "What were you thinking, for God's sake? Did you think that I am a coward who would give up on your love just because I became the target of public insults and disapproval? I swear on your life that even if everybody were to rise against me and slay my head with a sword, they couldn't sever my passionate desire for you. Should they spill my blood, the vapor emanating from it will be the vapor of my desire and love for you."

That evening, the girls recorded these five couplets as if they were treasures and spent the next couple of days constantly reciting them. Even though Râkım took the greatest pleasure from the way the girls read the Persian poems with their English accents, he also wanted to have them read the couplets eloquently; so after giving them a couplet, he'd spend five to ten days correcting their reading and pronunciation. In the end, the way these girls read the couplets in Persian was so beautiful as to make a human soul quiver.

Do you remember how last winter Mr. Ziklas asked Râkım to show them an example of an *alaturka* meal? You might have forgotten about it but Mr. Ziklas hadn't. He reminded Râkım of his old promise.

RÂKIM: It would be my pleasure, Sir! But there is a slight hitch.

MR. ZIKLAS: What is it?

RÂKIM: Since we're Muslims, our women hide away from men.

MR. ZIKLAS: Oh, I know! Although I assume you're not married.

RÂKIM: I'm not, but there are women in my house. What I'm trying to say is women aren't supposed to be present at an *alaturka* meal. Yet, if this meal will only be for your wife, Mrs. Ziklas, and the girls, they can participate in an *alaturka* meal in its entirety.

MR. ZIKLAS: I wanted this meal to be for them after all. Let them see it, and they will tell me about it afterwards.

RÂKIM: But there's another way to go about it according to *alaturka* culture.

MR. ZIKLAS: What is it?

RÂKIM: It's having an *alaturka* family meal where women and men dine together.

MR. ZIKLAS: Much better my friend, much better!

RÂKIM: However, in that case, you yourself can't see the women. You can only see a black Arab arm extending a shallow frying pan through the door.

MR. ZIKLAS: You mean my family will hide away from me?

RÂKIM: Not from you, from me!

MR. ZIKLAS: Oh, I see. That is the *alaturka* way. If we can modify that part, then let's proceed.

RÂKIM: In that case it won't be entirely *alaturka*.

MR. ZIKLAS: Oh, for God's sake, then make it entirely *alaturka* so that I can see what this is all about.

RÂKIM: Very well.

With that, they decided to arrange the meal for the coming Friday. When Râkım arrived at his house and told his nanny about this arrangement, poor Fedayi was surprised but gladly took on the added responsibility for Râkım Efendi's sake. Better still, there wouldn't be any evening revelry at this meal as the guests were coming for brunch.

How many days were there until Friday anyway? No matter how many days there were, they all passed and Friday arrived. Seeing that everything was ready and in order at his house, Râkım started the day early and headed out to the Ziklas household in Beyoğlu.

"Hey, shall we get going?" "Yes, let's go." As these words were exchanged, two carriages were being prepared. Mr. Ziklas and his eldest daughter got on the first one, and Mrs. Ziklas, their youngest daughter, and Râkım got on the other. They used the Azapkapısı, Galata, and Tophane route to get to Salıpazarı. Upon entering his house, Râkım exclaimed, "There shall be no one," and explained what this exclamation meant and why it was used. First, he showed Mr. Ziklas into the living room. After Mr. Ziklas observed the living room and complimented Râkım on his good taste, Râkım hid him away in Janan's room, which was more spacious as Janan's bed had been removed. Râkım left Mr. Ziklas there saying, "Now you are captive in here." Then, he received the mother and their daughters in the living room.

MRS. ZIKLAS: Where did Mr. Ziklas go?

RÂKIM: Miss, you are now forbidden from being together with him.

MRS. ZIKLAS: Oh come on now, really?

RÂKIM: Didn't you want the *alaturka* way?

When Janan appeared in front of the guests, Râkım had to introduce her to them; however, he couldn't make something up and say, "She is my sister," and he couldn't express himself thoroughly by giving only her name "Janan," so he was finally obliged to introduce her by saying, "She's my slave." He immediately went into the other room and sat with Monsieur Ziklas. In the living room, Mrs. Ziklas and the girls were astonished at Janan. They assumed that a slave would be tied up in a stable like an animal the way they are in America, so they couldn't comprehend what kind of a slave she was. On top of this, when Janan asked after their health in impeccable French, they were astonished, but pleased that this would help clarify the situation.

You know how the English are! When they are curious about something, they don't hold back from asking about it in great detail. For this reason they didn't only ask about when and why Janan became a slave but also about what her price had been. After Janan said, "My master bought me for a hundred liras," they were completely bewildered. When they noticed that she was wearing three to five hundred liras worth of diamonds, they were even more surprised and asked each other in English, "My dear, how could they sell such a beautiful girl for a hundred liras?" Finally, they also asked, "Do these diamonds belong to you?" Surprised and a bit embarrassed at the guests' overt and relentless questioning, Janan answered them saying that her master had given them to her as a gift.

Mrs. Ziklas liked Janan and admired the little girl's manners. Yes, even the girls appreciated her politeness and nice manners. Why? Who knows? They would converse by whispering into each other's ears, "Giving a slave that was bought for a hundred liras, five or six hundred liras worth of diamonds as a gift . . . How does that work?"

Meanwhile, in the other room, Râkım was describing to Mr. Ziklas the methods and rituals of an *alaturka* meal. Mr. Ziklas couldn't agree to being separated from his wife and children for another hour or two, so he reminded Râkım of his wish to mix some *alafranga* into this *alaturka* style and have his wife and children beside him.

Râkım informed Mrs. Ziklas and her daughters about this wish, which they all approved, and they joined Mr. Ziklas. They were amazed at everything they saw in Râkım's home. They even informed Mr. Ziklas about Janan. Margaret told him, "Father! So here they can buy a girl more beautiful than me for a hundred liras." When her father also expressed his amazement, Râkım said, "No Sir! She was worth a hundred liras at the time she was bought. Now, she would be worth somewhere between 1,500 and 2,000 liras." Even this surprised Mr. Ziklas, who said, "How strange! So there is a price even for people? How wonderful! If I sold my wife and daughters for 2,000 liras each, that would make 6,000 liras. Not bad, eh?"

RÂKIM: By all means! You should definitely do that! Now that the ladies have learned Turkish, they would make wonderful Turkish and Ottoman wives.

MARGARET: Would that be so terrible?

JAN: If I weren't going to be imprisoned in the house, I'd consent to being a Turkish wife.

RÂKIM: Janan, who isn't even a Turkish wife, but just a slave, isn't imprisoned in the house. She goes wherever she wants.

MARGARET: And father, the girl has a couple thousand shillings worth of diamonds on her.

RÂKIM: Do you see it now? How wonderful. You'd also have diamonds worth a
couple thousand liras.

MR. ZIKLAS: But Râkım Efendi . . . you describe slavery in such a way that soon
I'll want to be sold as a slave myself . . .

After this conversation, they had a good laugh together. As the girls
were curious to see Janan one more time, they took leave from their father
and went to sit next to her in the living room. Janan showed them the garden. She showed them everything: her flowers, pigeons, birds, two beautiful chickens, one rooster, and a lamb. The girls liked these animals very
much and regretted that although they were wealthy, they didn't possess
such pleasant things. Afterwards, they went into Râkım's personal room.
When they saw the library, they started poking around his books. They
opened every single book and looked over a couple of words in each.
Janan wasn't terribly surprised when she saw them reading Turkish for
she knew from her master that they could. The girls even looked at his col-
lection of treasured items. Later, they started looking around the drafts of
the novel that Râkım was in the process of writing; however, they couldn't
read his handwriting, as it was hastily written, thus a bit illegible. Finally,
they all sat down on the floor and started talking:

MARGARET: Aren't there any other rooms in this house?

JANAN: There is another room that way, where our nanny sleeps.

JAN: What nanny?

JANAN: She is an Arab that raised my master.

MARGARET: An Arab? Where is she now?

JANAN: She is getting things ready downstairs.

MARGARET: Is this Râkım Efendi's room?

JANAN: Yes.

JAN: Then where do *you* sleep?

JANAN: My room is the one where your father is sitting now.

MARGARET: No, no . . . that's not a bedroom. There are no beds in there!

JANAN: We removed it because you were coming.

JAN: No, that's not right.

JANAN: Why shouldn't it be right?

JAN: You are Râkım Efendi's wife.

JANAN (*blushing like a beet*): No, Mademoiselle! I am his slave.

MARGARET: No, no, it's not like that either. You are his "*concubine*"; what do they call it here . . . ah, odalisque. I know all about it, all of the Ottomans have odalisques.

JANAN (*even more embarrassed*): No, no! Our master doesn't do such things.

JAN: Or, does he not like you? But if he didn't like you, he wouldn't have given you that many diamonds. You are hiding something.

JANAN (*feeling quite bothered by their boldness*): He likes me, but not like an odalisque, he likes me like a sister.

MARGARET: Oh, please! Is it even possible to like one like a sister? You can hide it all you want. Congratulations. Râkım Efendi is very handsome, very smart, and very mature!

At this point in their conversation both of the English girls' attitudes changed. If you looked attentively at their faces, you'd see countless symptoms of jealousy. In fact, even if they themselves weren't aware of it, Janan understood it very well but couldn't make sense of why the girls took issue with her. She, too, expressed a certain hostility toward them.

Janan left the room to take care of some things. This time, the girls started talking among themselves.

JAN: You're right Margaret. This girl is Râkım Efendi's odalisque.

MARGARET: Isn't that obvious? Didn't you see how she blushed?

JAN: Yet, she is a beautiful girl, isn't she?

MARGARET: Oh, what is beautiful about her?

JAN: Oh, come on, she *is* beautiful; however . . .

MARGARET: However, what?

JAN: I'm trying to say she doesn't deserve Râkım Efendi.

MARGARET: If you think she is beautiful, then why do you say she doesn't deserve him?

JAN: She deserves him for her beauty; however, she is still a slave! Where is the harm in that, though? Let her be a slave. She is a slave; yet, do you see how happy she is? She has become Râkım Efendi's odalisque. She is beautiful, and Râkım Efendi is beautiful. Both beautiful and mature.

MARGARET: It seems like you are also jealous.

JAN: Why would I be jealous?

MARGARET: My, this is just like a dream! I'd want to be a slave like this. If I were Râkım Efendi's odalisque, I would have him read Persian poems to me night and day.

JAN: Let's see if he shows us the same regard that he shows this poor slave. And who is she? We . . .

MARGARET: Let me tell you something, Jan. Râkım Efendi certainly likes this slave very much. See, as he told us, he taught her Turkish and then French.

JAN: Besides, did you see the piano outside?

MARGARET: I did but how we do know if she's the one who plays it?

JAN: Who else would? Râkım Efendi doesn't know how to play the piano.

MARGARET: Do you see? This means that he found someone to teach her how to play the piano. What was he saying just now? This girl was worth a hundred liras when she was purchased. He said that she'd be worth two thousand liras now. See, he finds her so valuable because he educated and polished her in this way.

We included the details of these conversations between Jan, Margaret, and Janan because we thought that they were necessary for our story. The conversation in the other room between Râkım and the Ziklas couple touched on this and that. Afterwards, the girls returned to the living room with Janan and sat in front of the piano. At this point, Mr. Ziklas's pleasure heightened. They played both *alafranga* and *alaturka* tunes. They played their favorite song, "O morning breeze, do not blow," twice. Finally, mealtime arrived and Râkım entered the room bearing a short, round dinner table with folding legs, a round brass tray, a tablecloth, and napkins. He then showed Mr. Ziklas all the accessories of an *alaturka* table: the pouch for the silverware, breadbasket, salt and pepper shakers, and the floor poufs. The crazy Englishman studied each of them one by one and was surprised at the detailed information he received about them all.

Everybody sat down at the table. They ate the soup in keeping with tradition. Later, just as Râkım had described, a black Arab arm extended the frying pan filled with stew through the doorway. Mr. Ziklas was so surprised and curious that he attempted to stand up and look at the Arab.

The girls had already leaped up from their seats but sat back down when their mother intervened.

People always laugh when they see a Turk who's never eaten at an *alafranga* table eat in *alafranga* style. For instance, it really amuses people to see Turks who can't manage to cut their meat with a knife and instead pick it up and shred it with their hands before using a fork. On the other hand, it makes people split their sides laughing to see an Englishman, who has never eaten in the *alaturka* way, eat in *alaturka* style. The way the guests ate today made them laugh at themselves! For example, as soon as Mr. Ziklas dipped his finger all the way into the frying pan, which was filled with boiling hot stew, he pulled his arm away in pain as quick as lightning, hitting his wife, who was sitting right next to him, with his elbow, and knocking the poor woman over. You couldn't have stopped laughing if you'd seen this yourself.

Anyway, they finished the meal, and it was late afternoon by the time the Ziklas family returned home. Mr. and Mrs. Ziklas were enchanted with the *alaturka* way of life just as Madame Josephine had been a couple days ago. The girls, on the other hand, returned regretting that they had ever gone in the first place.

Why?

Who knows? We only know that they left the place feeling jealous of everything they observed about Janan. If you wish, you can attribute this to their childishness, or, if you wish . . .

Chapter 9

THINGS CONTINUED ALONG AS USUAL. That is, Râkım continued to fulfill his duties as a translator, writer, and teacher. If there was an apparent modification in the state of affairs, it was the slight change in the way the English girls treated him.

For example, although Râkım had met with them several times over the past week or so, the girls, especially the eldest, Jan, continued to act in a way that suggested they might have developed a grudge or some kind of animosity toward their dear teacher. It wasn't possible for this attitude to go unnoticed; in fact, Râkım thought that perhaps he wasn't needed there anymore. As a result, he canceled the lesson one night on purpose. However, when he came back the next day, the girls asked him why he had canceled the lesson and what had prevented him from coming, and said that they were bored in his absence. Jan said, "Don't you know that we enjoy your lessons more than anything else? We forget all about our hearts' troubles thanks to your lessons." As they had gone this far in the discussion, Râkım wanted to get to the bottom of his suspicions. Yet, he cut it short, thinking, "One declaration leads to another, and these declarations then provoke undesirable revelations."

Afterwards, the girls' demeanor changed. At the end of the lesson, they did nothing but inquire about Janan's situation. Jan competed with her little sister in these interrogations. They asked all sorts of questions, including questions about Janan's education and even the purpose she served in the house!

Râkım didn't need to think too hard to realize the motivations behind these questions; however, since he found these motivations unsettling, he put aside his suspicions and came up with an appropriate answer to their questions. For instance, when they asked him what purpose Janan currently served in the house, he said, "My nanny is very lonesome. And doesn't somebody need to manage the household? That's what Janan does, she manages the household."

Yet, Jan's curiosity was such that she remained unsatisfied with these perfunctory answers. She seemed bewildered when she heard Râkım's answer and responded, "How strange that the *femme de chambre* (chambermaid) is such a young, beautiful, and bejeweled girl, and that she wears three to five hundred liras worth of diamonds!" Râkım's suspicions were only heightened by her puzzled reaction.

It has been three months since Râkım hosted the English family at his house. During this time, Janan has grown more independent in front of her master. For example, from time to time, Nanny's eyes unwittingly caught a glimpse of Râkım's arms around Janan's neck in the living room. If Nanny were a curious woman, she could have seen some even more pleasant scenes. However, these scenes were enough for her to know that Râkım—her son, master; in short, her everything in this world—had found bliss. Besides, Janan didn't hide anything from her nanny and would have told her about it anyway.

Oh my! For God's sake, what kind of incidents would she tell her about?

To be honest, if you want the truth, Janan didn't recount every detail to her nanny. According to what Janan said, her master would summon her at night to have a heart-to-heart conversation. The occasional black marks observed on Janan's face and neck shouldn't be considered signs of dishonor for a female slave in Janan's position, but rather signs of honor.

Bravo, Râkım! He really was happy!

Yes, he was! But for Râkım, all happiness was destined to arrive mixed with a few tears; this happiness, too, had come in return for a fair amount of tears.

Now that Janan had met the English girls that Râkım had been teaching until midnight twice a week, she was consumed with all sorts of suspicions. When Râkım returned to his house at night after these lessons, he could see signs of Janan's distress. Her eyes were red, eyelashes still wet, her voice trembled, and sometimes she was even short of breath. Wasn't Râkım supposed to dispel poor Janan's anguish out of his love for her? Oh, how can a lover dispel such grief when away from his beloved? Of course by offering her compliments and expressions of his sincerity, love, and loyalty. The signs of Râkım's love were clearly visible on Janan's face and neck.

Do you ever recall Felâtun Bey?

Forget that frivolous fool!

But don't say that! Half of this story belongs to him. We need to know what happened to him over the course of these last three months.

Paying for his accommodation at Hotel J—— began to seem excessive and exorbitant.

Well, well! So does this now mean that he started pulling himself together?

Yes! They say that money and reason don't go together. Felâtun Bey was a perfect illustration of this statement. After he had engaged in all kinds of reckless spending and lost about seventy-five percent of his fortune, reason began to replace his lost wealth. In order to reduce his expenditures so to speak, he rented a house in Büyükdere, a suitable choice for the season, and moved his madame into the house.

Now let us turn our glances to the English girls—yes, to the English girls. After all, their situation has already begun to preoccupy us. It most certainly has. The poor elder sister—Jan, that is—fell ill. What kind of illness? Nobody knew. There were no apparent symptoms! It started with melancholy. She was restless. Even the Turkish books that she loved so dearly and never stopped reading failed to entertain her. Concerned about Jan's condition, her parents, with their doctor's approbation, would try to entertain her by taking her for a stroll in their carriage down to Taksim and into the countryside. However, even this couldn't distract the girl. When her father said, "Come on, my dear girl, here, our carriage is ready, let's go for a ride," the girl consented wearily. If her father asked, "Well, where shall we go today?" the girl would say, "Wherever you wish. It makes no difference to me." When she said this, her father realized that even if he were to take her to heaven, it would be to no avail.

You know what happens to a person who suffers from this illness, don't you? They become listless, turn pale, and lose weight. This is exactly what happened to Jan. This sturdy English girl, who Felâtun had likened to a carrot and a beet, turned as colorless as a potato. Her lips blanched and paled. Those blue eyes became hollow and looked like worn turquoise.

Râkım felt sorry when he saw the poor girl in this state. Whenever he ran into an expert doctor, he'd describe her symptoms and ask for the doctor's opinion. After thinking about it for a while, the doctor would inquire who the patient was and Râkım would say that she was a dear acquaintance. The doctor would then reply, "It's all right, she'll be fine," with an expression that didn't quite match his words.

They even had to cancel the Turkish lesson once. For a while, the family sent the girl to their friends' house in Kadıköy for a change of scenery. However, the poor girl's anguish only increased during her stay there. She wrote a letter home, to her sister that is, asking her to send her poetry journal. In the margin of the letter, she added that she "would be happy if Râkım Efendi came to check on her from time to time." Margaret sent her sister the journal and showed the note to her father. By know you should know that her father would do anything within his power to please Jan. He immediately sent a man to invite Râkım over and Râkım made his way to the Ziklas household at once.

MR. ZIKLAS: My dear Râkım Efendi! I have a request for you. Our Jan says that she'd be pleased if you could visit her sometime. However, if this service will keep you from your work, don't be afraid, I'm happy to recompense you.

RÂKIM: Not at all, Mr. Ziklas. Thinking so much about one's own profit might be a European thing to do but it certainly isn't Ottoman. Absolutely. I'll go tomorrow.

MR. ZIKLAS: Could you possibly go tonight? Although there won't be any ferries now, you can hire a little boat.

RÂKIM: At this time of the night? Wouldn't I be disturbing the household?

MR. ZIKLAS: Ah, you're right! I'm just so worried about this girl.

RÂKIM: We all are, Sir.

Râkım found himself in Kadıköy early the next morning. When Jan saw her teacher, she smiled slightly and this expression made the host family so happy that they immediately wrote about it to her parents. This is what parenthood is like! It was just before noon when Jan's parents and sister showed up in Kadıköy, for the news of Jan's having smiled was a great blessing for them.

Margaret found her sister with Hafez's collected works in her hands. Jan cheered up when she saw her parents, and everyone was pleased to see her in this happy state. After sitting with her until evening, they were even more delighted when Jan expressed her desire to go home with them; so they all returned together.

So when she came back . . .

Indeed, her condition worsened soon afterwards. On the third day after her return home, her demeanor altered entirely and she took to her bed.

Doctor Z——, who had been treating her all along, couldn't come up with a firm diagnosis, and for lack of evidence, settled on tuberculosis. Finally, one night as the doctor was reading ancient history, he happened upon a story and decided to act in accordance with it.

What was the story?

What use is the story? Look at what he did and you'll understand. He went to the Ziklas household the next morning and asked who the girl saw on a regular basis. Mr. Ziklas couldn't think of more than two or three people apart from his own family, Râkım and the servants. Doctor Z—— requested that all of those people gather there around mid-afternoon that same day; he also recommended that these people be kept in a separate room away from the patient.

At mid-afternoon, the doctor found all these people waiting in the room just as he had requested. He asked Mrs. Ziklas to send them into Jan's room one by one and joined Mr. Ziklas next to her bed. The desperate girl was in an extremely weak state. The doctor and her father placed their hands on the girl's heart and noticed how weakly her heart beat. The first person to enter the room was the son of their Italian neighbors. When the girl saw him, she tried to put her own troubles aside and asked the boy how he was doing, "How are you Monsieur Cyrano, doing well?" Even though Cyrano approached the bed, held her hand, and asked how she was doing, there was no change in Jan's heartbeat, which appeared to be fairly at ease. At the doctor's signal, Cyrano exited the room and this time a married Greek neighbor entered. There were still no extraordinary movements in her heart. No changes were observed at entrance of the French coachman either. Râkım was the fourth to enter and even as he made his way in through the door, her heart started beating fiercely just as it does when one wakes up from sleep!

The doctor immediately jabbed Mr. Ziklas with his elbow. Mr. Ziklas winked to say, "I see."

This wasn't the only discernible change in Jan when Râkım entered. A series of expressions of joy and happiness appeared on her face. She exchanged greetings with her teacher more keenly than she did with anyone else. She wanted to rise and sit up in her bed. And so she did! The doctor didn't see any need to continue with his experiment, so he allowed everyone to enter the room and sit together. Meanwhile, in another room, the doctor and Mr. Ziklas had the following conversation:

DOCTOR: Did you understand what caused the change in her heart as her teacher entered the room?

MR. ZIKLAS: How couldn't I? I feared that the heart under my hand was about to jump out of her chest. Ah, how fragile she is!

DOCTOR: Sir, don't get me wrong. But her illness is the illness of love and desire.

MR. ZIKLAS: If that's the case, then she is in love with Râkım Efendi. Am I right?

DOCTOR: There, you said it yourself.

MR. ZIKLAS: Well . . . what's the cure for this?

DOCTOR: There is no cure, Sir.

MR. ZIKLAS: What's going to happen to her then?

DOCTOR: To be honest, I shouldn't be saying this since you are her father but there is nothing left to hide here, so I'll just say it. This girl won't survive in this condition for another two months.

MR. ZIKLAS: For God's sake, Monsieur Z——!

DOCTOR: I am telling you what I see! Well, there *is* a cure for this but I doubt if it's realizable.

MR. ZIKLAS: I'll make it happen!

DOCTOR: Would you marry your girl to Monsieur Râkım?

MR. ZIKLAS (*consumed by boundless excitement, after some silence*): What should I do . . . watch her die? If it were up to me, I would marry her to Râkım.

DOCTOR: Well, it's a possibility. It's your decision. If you want, we can forbid the teacher from any contact with the girl.

MR. ZIKLAS: Would it help?

DOCTOR: No! But she might die a week earlier and be freed. You should have thought about this before. You shouldn't have allowed such a young teacher to get near your girls in the first place.

MR. ZIKLAS: Don't you know Râkım Efendi?

DOCTOR: I didn't notice any change in Râkım's expression that would indicate love or romantic interest. It seems as if he pitied her, almost like a brother.

MR. ZIKLAS: I know Râkım to be this way as well and I trust him completely. I mean, Râkım has never done anything to realize her hopes.

DOCTOR: I agree with you. However, a man doesn't have to say anything to a girl for her to fall in love with him. Do I need to say more? If your daughter and Râkım Efendi had a mutual love for each other and if they expressed this love, then this illness wouldn't have stricken her. Instead of this illness, she would have ended up with an illness of indecency. However . . .

MR. ZIKLAS: You are absolutely right, Monsieur Z——. I have no reason to believe that Râkım had any such designs on her. My desperate girl brought this on herself; she is killing herself. Let's see. If I can convince her, her mother, and Râkım, I will marry her to him. It's better than killing her . . .

DOCTOR: If that were to happen, we might well hope for her recovery.

There, this was how the examination was carried out that day; however, neither the girls nor Râkım, nor even Mrs. Ziklas had any knowledge concerning the hidden intent behind this examination. That night Mr. Ziklas informed his wife about the real intent behind the examination and told her that the only way to cure their daughter's illness was to marry her to Râkım. Oh, imagine her trepidation, distress, and opposition! She rejected it once and for all. She concluded that they needed to resign themselves to her death and asked her husband how he could bear the shame of marrying their daughter to someone else when the girls had so many cousins. Especially to a Turk and, what's worse, her teacher.

Oh poor Mrs. Ziklas! Her decision didn't sit well with her soul. How can any mother consent to her daughter's death? A couple hours later, she realized how flawed her decision had been and, crying, came to the same conclusion her husband had.

We already told you that Râkım had no knowledge of the hidden intent behind the examination. We wonder if Râkım had any idea that he was the cause of the girl's illness. Absolutely not! He did recognize that Jan was jealous of Janan when she questioned him about her but he couldn't imagine the possibility that this jealousy stemmed from her hidden desire and love for him. Hence, all of the sadness he felt for this poor patient stemmed from his sincere fondness for her. He returned home after the examination dispirited and in great dismay. When his nanny and Janan inquired, Râkım told them that Jan was ill and on her deathbed. That night Janan, out of genuine compassion, expressed pity for the young girl on her deathbed, yet she also ventured to ask Râkım about the reason for his intense concern.

RÂKIM: My God! Keep on asking and you will make me even more suspicious!
JANAN (*fearfully*): No, Sir, I don't suspect anything! I just see you very sad, that's all.
RÂKIM: Tell me, how can I not be sad? How can one not feel sorry for a healthy young girl on her deathbed?

There, you see, Râkım's fondness for Jan owed solely to his humanity and compassion. Have you also noticed that Janan has grown more audacious in front of Râkım?

The next morning, Mr. Ziklas's servant came again and invited Râkım back to their house. Râkım immediately inquired about Jan's condition but what could this man possible say? Isn't "a little better" just a standard phrase?

Râkım got up and made his way directly to Beyoğlu with no other thought in his mind. He found Mr. Ziklas and the doctor, Monsieur Z——, together in a room, so, naturally, he joined them. After asking about the patient's condition, receiving some kind of an answer, and talking about this and that, the doctor asked:

DOCTOR: My young man! Do you know why we invited you here today?
RÂKIM: What's the matter, Monsieur Z——?

DOCTOR: You appear to be the cause of our patient's illness.

RÂKIM (*unable to conceal his anxiety although without a full grasp of what was happening*): How so, Monsieur Z——?

DOCTOR: Just as you appear to be the cause of her illness, we now also expect you to cure it.

RÂKIM (*finally realizing the truth and feeling distressed*): For God's sake Monsieur Z——! Are you about to tell me something that's never crossed my mind before?

MR. ZIKLAS (*crying*): It's all right, Monsieur Râkım, it's all right. We're going to tell you something that has never crossed your mind before. The thing that's never occurred to you has been preoccupying Jan for some time now.

Râkım went ice cold and turned white as a sheet.

DOCTOR: My friend, this girl is suffering from love and affection—love and affection she feels for you. Yesterday's examination proved this.

RÂKIM: Mr. Ziklas! Monsieur Z——! I assure you, I'll swear on anything you like that I didn't know about any of this until this very second and I still can't believe it.

MR. ZIKLAS AND DOCTOR: Yes, we know.

RÂKIM (*without interrupting*): Now, I am searching my soul and in all honesty, I can't find any trace of such feelings for her. Still, I did love Jan. And I say proudly that I do love her. I also love Margaret. Yet, I love them like my children, sisters, or sincere friends.

MR. ZIKLAS: I know my dear boy, I know.

RÂKIM (*without interrupting*): They also love me, yet I swear on my faith and honor that I've never heard a single syllable, never seen a single move from them that would substantiate what you're saying.

DOCTOR: We, I mean the whole family, know this, my good friend. We don't doubt you. Yet, this girl suffers from love. And this love is for you. Left in this condition, she'll die. Her only chance is if you agree to provide the cure.

RÂKIM: How can I help?

DOCTOR: We are doing our best to save this young girl from the dark claws of death, so please don't reproach us for what we're about to propose. Mr. Ziklas wants to make you Jan's groom.

RÂKIM (*with trepidation and palpitation*): Who? Me?

MR. ZIKLAS (*crying*): Yes, my son, you! What else can I do? Nobody is to blame here . . . not me, not you, and certainly not the girl. Who wouldn't love an angel like you, my son? Your beauty, education, wisdom, righteousness, and noble attitude! All of these would make a girl fall for you.

RÂKIM (*with increased anxiety*): Please, Mr. Ziklas!

DOCTOR: This is how we'll do it. I suppose that your religion also permits it, and Mr. Ziklas is a liberal man.

MR. ZIKLAS: What are you saying for God's sake? I am ready to agree to my girl's conversion to Islam. Is there anything bad in Islam? Don't we all pray to one God? Is there any difference between our beliefs? Jesus and Mary would allow her to change her religion and convert to Islam in order to save her from death.

RÂKIM: Sir, these are all details. But . . .

DOCTOR: No need for any "but's." You should make this sacrifice for us. Though I have to say that becoming a groom in the Ziklas family is not a sacrifice, it's an honor. It would even work in your favor!

RÂKIM: Of course, all that is true. I wouldn't even deem myself suitable for such an honor. However, there is something else. I'm already married.

MR. ZIKLAS: Married?

RÂKIM: Yes, see, the female slave you met happens to be my wife.

MR. ZIKLAS: I would like your permission to doubt what you're saying is true, Monsieur Râkım.

RÂKIM: No, Sir, please believe me when I say it's true.

MR. ZIKLAS: Râkım Efendi! Râkım Efendi! I am offering you half of my fortune because all I have belongs to my two daughters and nobody else. If you save this girl from her impending death, I'll offer you a fortune of around 300,000 British liras, not to mention kinship ties with me.

(Janan's ears must be ringing!)

DOCTOR: What joy!

MR. ZIKLAS: That girl, that female slave of yours can't be more than a concubine anyway.

DOCTOR: What would be the problem even if she were his lawfully wed wife? The Ottomans can easily divorce their wives and marry another.

RÂKIM (*after having listened to these words with great astonishment*): Mr. Ziklas! I'm a poor man. I earn my bread and butter by writing petitions and other kinds of documents and by tutoring. What I'm trying to say is that the offer you're making to a man like me is a dream. Especially since I wouldn't give up your friendship if I were offered millions! However, I've lost my heart to Janan. When she was a slave in the house, I was happy making her happy. How could I possibly make Janan cry for lack of money or other sorts of happiness? I beg you Sir, let me kiss your hand! Release me from this offer. If you order me not to come to your house again, I won't.

Do you know how surprised Mr. Ziklas and the doctor were upon hearing Râkım speak these words? The doctor wanted to attribute Râkım's contentedness to stupidity. He thought, "What a fool! At least pretend to accept Ziklas's offer, and then go have fun with your Janan."

Are you astonished to hear this? If so, then there is more: The same idea also occurred to Mr. Ziklas. He said, "At least take my daughter but continue to love Janan in secret and hide it from my daughter!" Now, if you want, you can feel more astonished. Or if you really want, you can also interpret this as Râkım's stupidity. But Râkım didn't accept this proposal and said, "Mr. Ziklas, you're making me such an offer that, if it weren't coming from the pain and sorrow that's been plaguing you, I'd take that as an insult. I couldn't indulge in deceit and dishonesty even if I were offered this whole world as a reward. How on earth could I lie to Jan and say, 'I love you?'"

The tears running down Râkım's cheeks proved that he was completely serious in his sentiments. Mr. Ziklas and Monsieur Z—— thought desperately for a while. The looks on their faces suggested that none of the possibilities that had crossed their minds were feasible. They all stood up and began pacing about the room. Finally, Râkım broke the silence by saying, "Mr. Ziklas, I ask for your forgiveness if I have committed any impertinence. With your permission, I'll take my leave." Mr. Ziklas hugged Râkım, kissed him, and said, "Where are you going, my son, where? You didn't commit any impertinence. We did! You didn't show us anything but your good morals, contentedness, honor, loyalty, valor, bravery, and generosity. You are and will always be my greatest friend in this world."

Even the doctor was moved when he saw the old man in this state. Finally, the doctor proffered another possibility that just crossed his mind and changed the mood in the room:

DOCTOR: There is one last resort.

MR. ZIKLAS: What Monsieur Z——, what is it?

DOCTOR: I don't know what Monsieur Râkım will say to this.

RÂKIM (*with great sorrow*): Go ahead, Monsieur Doctor.

DOCTOR: Let's go tell the girl the good news that you love her. In fact, let's go and
inform her that you and her father have been having this conversation and if
she pulls herself together soon, he'll marry her to you. From what I've seen,
the most important challenge for a girl in this condition is the inability to tell
anyone about her trouble. If we bring it up ourselves, we'll raise her boldness
and her hopes.

MR. ZIKLAS: What do you say, Râkım Efendi?

RÂKIM: If it were up to me, I wouldn't agree to this. However, if this measure will
do any good, then I won't object.

DOCTOR: You shouldn't object. We know what good will come from it.

Upon the doctor's suggestion, the doctor and Râkım stood up and went to her bedside without Mr. Ziklas. As usual, an invigoration, a joy was observed in the girl when she saw Râkım.

They asked after each other's health. In fact, Jan even asked after Janan. Do you suppose that Râkım gave her the correct answer after the words they had exchanged in the other room? If you suppose that he gave Jan a clue about his love for Janan, you'd be making a mistake. With all the sincerity in his heart, he told her that Janan was in good health. In the meantime, the doctor spoke briefly with great sincerity.

DOCTOR: Mademoiselle Jan! I'll tell you something only if you assure me that you
won't be surprised.

JAN (*turning a little pale*): What is it, Monsieur Doctor?

DOCTOR: Monsieur Râkım told me about a secret of his. As you know, doctors and
priests know about all sorts of secrets, but keeping those secrets is also . . .

JAN (*with a slight change in her expression*): I don't understand what you're saying,
Sir.

DOCTOR: This is only youthfulness, not a dishonor! For you, Râkım Efendi has
a . . .

JAN (*changing all together*): I understand. But I'm surprised. Râkım Efendi loves
me like a sister . . .

DOCTOR: No, no, amorous love is stronger than the love felt for a sibling. Isn't that
right, Monsieur Râkım?

RÂKIM (*with an obligatory expression*): Oh! It is, Doctor, it is! I'm unable to bring
myself to say it, I can't say a word, and I can't express myself. You say it for me
then. If she hasn't noticed what happens to me when I see her in the sickbed
like this, then you tell her.

JAN: How strange! Râkım Efendi, are you telling the truth?

RÂKIM: I am indeed!

JAN: Until now, I never supposed that you were afflicted with this illness.

DOCTOR: Yes, yes. Since the day you entered your sickbed, his illness has gotten
worse. Yet, this is not really what we're here to tell you, Mademoiselle.

JAN (*gathering her strength considerably*): Wait, there's more?

DOCTOR: There's more, Mademoiselle. We've also told your father about this
situation.

JAN (*more agitated than before*): My father?

RÂKIM: Yes, your father!

DOCTOR: At Râkım Efendi's insistence, I informed him about this. Islam allows
you to get married and still keep your own religion. Your father consented
to it. He accepted Râkım Efendi's many merits. In fact, he was going to come
and make the marriage proposal himself; however, you know how it is to be
a father; in case you'd feel embarrassed or he'd feel embarrassed, he assigned
this honorable duty to me, trusting my knowledge of this secret.

JAN (*with a bitter smile that could pierce a person's heart*): How strange! But how
could *you* believe all this?

DOCTOR: I fear that you don't want to accept Râkım Efendi.

JAN: Just wait and call my father!

Râkım quickly exited the room and summoned Mr. Ziklas. Before
they came back, the doctor managed to say, "I'm telling the truth, mademoiselle. This man is going crazy with his love for you. Your father has

shown mercy to Râkım and agreed to your marriage. It's all up to you now." Mr. Ziklas and Râkım arrived.

JAN (*with remarkable embarrassment*): My dear father, Monsieur Doctor is saying certain things!

MR. ZIKLAS: Yes, my dear daughter. Go ahead and say whatever you want. There are no strangers here.

RÂKIM: If you want, I can step out.

JAN (*again, with a bitter smile*): No need. (*to herself*): How will it remain hidden, that secret that is the subject of gatherings?

When Râkım heard this line, he trembled with an incomprehensible sorrow.

JAN (*continuing*): Yes, Father dear! The doctor said what needed to be said. I didn't believe this whole thing to be possible. And then he asked whether I love Râkım Efendi or not. However, when he left the room, he added that Râkım Efendi was going crazy with love for me.

MR. ZIKLAS: That's good, my dear! What's your answer?

JAN: Okay, so here is my answer: I love Râkım. He loves me, too. He does; however, the way he loves me is not the way I love him. He loves me like a sister. I love him the way his female slave Janan loves him. I love him, but, oh, what's the use?

As the poor girl said these words, everyone's eyes filled with tears: the poor girl's, her father's, the doctor's, and Râkım's.

JAN: Râkım, Râkım! If you place your lips on my lips, I'll receive eternal life / At the moment I give up the sweet ghost through my lips.

Upon hearing this couplet, Râkım burst into a flood of tears. Seeing Râkım cry, the old father began crying, too. The doctor, on the other hand, froze like ice and stood fixed to the spot.

JAN: Dear Father, if there were a way to carry out the decision you made, I'd return to life and rise. Hear me when I say, Râkım doesn't love me as I love him. He loves me like his sister. If he loved me the way I love him, he definitely would have shown a sign of it by now. Even when girls talk about such private matters among themselves, they would utter words that would make one another blush. But Râkım never uttered any such words when he was with us. I never spoke a word to him about it. I only thought to myself: With your stony heart, will it ever take effect one night / My predawn fiery sighs and burning laments.

MR. ZIKLAS: See, that's good, my dear. Just like you, although Râkım loved you, he didn't say anything. Isn't that so, Râkım Efendi?

Râkım had no strength left to answer the question.

JAN: It's useless, my dear father! With Janan in the picture, whatever you do will be useless. In fact, even if Râkım, out of pity for me, were to agree to do what you are asking, I wouldn't agree. If I'm going to die, then let me die. I can't agree to cause the death of a desperate girl for the sake of my own happiness.

The atmosphere in the room changed and even the doctor started sobbing. Fortunately, the girl's mother wasn't present. If she had been, there would undoubtedly have been more scenes. As for Jan, she stopped crying. Looking at Râkım, she said,

JAN: "The soul that is at the end of its rope plans to see you, shall it hold out or shall it let go. What is your command?" What I mean to say, my dear father, is I am grateful for the compassion you showed me, and to you also Monsieur Doctor. Thank you, too, Râkım Efendi, for you probably had a big battle with your heart in order to accept to take part in such a ruse. The sacrifice you made means a lot to me. Oh, I'd face up to any shame in order to get a single kiss from you right now. However, I've decided to go to heaven longing and yearning for your kiss. I hope to receive God's compassion this way.

No one had the strength to endure the gathering any longer. The doctor was the first one to manifest his weakness and leave. Râkım followed him out of the room and Jan's desperate father looked at her face forlornly for a while. When he left, he sent for her mother and younger sister to join her.

All right, they all exited the room but did they begin another conversation? Was that even possible! They all just stared at one another like mutes, expressing their wishes silently. Each of them communicated their agony silently with their eyes. What did Jan's mother and sister talk about at her bedside?

Well see, we don't know about that. We only know that Râkım realized that he didn't need to stay in this mournful house any longer, so at some point he snuck out and left. On the verge of crying with Jan's anguished condition on his mind, he started down the Kumbaracı Yokuşu with his head lowered.

Chapter 10

POOR JAN LEFT RÂKIM feeling extraordinarily sad. So much so that although Râkım had no amorous feelings for Jan, it seems as though they were on the verge of emerging. "What happened to this poor girl? She has begun to look almost ghostly. Honest to God, it's hard not to like her. Reading Persian is her particular skill. Ah, see, isn't it Hafez's poetry that brought her to this state? I couldn't predict that it would have had such an impact. How she listened to and absorbed the most passionate couplets with a fire in her heart! Now I realize she was poisoning herself with them. Alas, poor Jan, alas! If something happens to her, I swear I'll die." Thinking these thoughts, he went all the way down to Hendekbaşı.

Who do you suppose he ran across there?

Felâtun Bey!

Oh, no, put that waster aside!

How can we? How can we abandon the fellow who is a partner to half of our story?

We should never have included him in this story in the first place.

We shouldn't have . . . but we already did. Besides, where is this animosity towards Felâtun Bey coming from? Is it that you can't stand his *alafranga* ways? If Felâtun Bey didn't exist, how could the mayonnaise incident have occurred? What about Hotel J——? Would it be able to host such a rich *alafranga* Ottoman if not for Felâtun Bey? Would the two bands have played in front of the lady's carriage in Kağıthane?

What good is it if he's going to rack and ruin?

It's all right! We assure you that he is not going to go rack and ruin anymore. He can't anyway!

We fear that his money . . .

Instead of worrying, listen to this:

FELÂTUN: Well, well, brother! God bless you! Gentility changes a person! One stops seeing old friends.

RÂKIM (*at a loss for words due to his sorrow*): Not at all, brother! I am very distressed today. You know Ziklas' girl, right? I mean the elder one, Jan?

FELÂTUN: Yes, Jan, who makes one want to steal her heart, right? That impossible beauty, if only I hadn't made the mistake of embracing her mother in the dark!

RÂKIM: Stop it, for God's sake! The poor girl is fighting for her life.

FELÂTUN: What's wrong?

RÂKIM: How should I know what's wrong? Maybe she has tuberculosis. Doctors say it is lovesickness.

FELÂTUN: There, you see? This is as good as philosophers like you can do. You say, "we should protect our honor, we should protect our decency," and give such young girls tuberculosis and then abandon them. Would she have gotten tuberculosis if she'd been interested in me? She'd be fit as a fiddle!

RÂKIM (*lethargically*): My good man, let's leave this aside. The poor girl will be a goner one of these days. Tell me, what are *you* up to? How are things with Pauline?

FELÂTUN: Since you made me stop talking about Jan, I also propose that you stop talking about Pauline.

RÂKIM: Oh? Why is that?

FELÂTUN: Because I broke up with her.

RÂKIM (*anxiously*): How come?

FELÂTUN: Stop talking about that slut, for God's sake!

RÂKIM: So that coquettish Pauline is a slut now?

FELÂTUN: Malicious courtesan! She left after robbing me blind and ruining me.

RÂKIM: Robbing you blind?

FELÂTUN: That's right!

RÂKIM: At least it wasn't more than a couple thousand liras, huh?

FELÂTUN: A couple thousand? More like sixteen thousand!

RÂKIM (*alarmed*): What? How much was your whole fortune anyway?

FELÂTUN (*tearily*): She took everything I had! Oh, my friend, you told me the right thing to do but what's the use now? If I knew then what I know now, I would've known what to do.

RÂKIM: So . . . what are you going to do now?

FELÂTUN: Now I am crying over spilled milk . . . but there is no point. I also fell out with my brother-in-law. I tell you, now I understand how things work in this world! Now I see that brothers-in-law do not accept penniless in-laws, and sisters do not accept penniless brothers. (*More tears welled in his eyes.*)

RÂKIM: It can't go on like this, right? You've surely thought of a solution.

FELÂTUN: I realized that I have only one true friend in this world. All the favors I've done finally bore fruit. You know our —— Bey, right?

RÂKIM: Yes!

FELÂTUN: Well, I've taken refuge in his mercy. He'll be able to arrange for me to be appointed as a provincial governor. I am really hoping and counting on it to work out.

RÂKIM: God bless you, brother! That would make me happy, too. Please tell me if I can do anything for you, but . . .

As soon as Râkım uttered these words, Felâtun looked at his face, gave him a bitter smile, and walked away without saying goodbye. Did this trouble Râkım now? Let's not get into it.

Why should this trouble Râkım? Felâtun should have opened his eyes earlier and shouldn't have allowed a slut to swindle him of his fortune. Didn't he used to turn up his nose at Râkım?

Yes! You're right about that. However, a man like Râkım would never be easy about anybody's humiliation or destruction. He would be troubled even if the person caught in such a state of destruction were his enemy.

This wasn't the only thing that troubled him when he came home that evening: there was also the question of Jan's illness. That night he didn't utter a single word and couldn't find the strength to eat. Her master's distress made Janan sick at heart. Given the unusual state of affairs, the poor girl couldn't bring herself to open her mouth and remained in front of Râkım with her head down. When he barked orders at Janan requesting things like cigarettes and coffee, he sounded almost like an overbearing janissary cleaning his knife after shedding the blood of a victim. Janan couldn't make up her mind as to whether she ought to cry or not and after everybody retired to their rooms, she cried long and feverishly in her own bed.

What happened to that Râkım who used to work with strict discipline and function like a chronometer? The next day, he was at a loss about where to go and what to do. Saying, "I'll get up now; I'll get dressed now; I'll go now but where shall I go; what work should I do?" Râkım remained stuck at home until mid-afternoon and eventually resigned himself to staying home for the rest of the day. Toward evening he got out the half-filled *rakı* bottle left over from the night of their dinner with Josephine, poured himself some, and began drinking. Even though Râkım sat Janan in front of the piano, she took no pleasure from playing as she saw no sign of joy on her master's face.

What if we said that Josephine showed up at the door! Apparently, that was their lesson day. Râkım greeted her. As it was in her nature to be cheerful and sassy, she greeted both Râkım and Janan with a thousand smiles and much jolliness. Both of them received Josephine's greetings coldly. Josephine was bewildered. She couldn't make any sense of this cold treatment.

JOSEPHINE: What is this? I see this house, which is always so happy, full of grief tonight. I hope nothing is wrong!

RÂKIM: No, thank God we don't have any cause for grief.

JOSEPHINE: Your words and your heart are not speaking the same language. I fear that Janan might have upset you.

JANAN (*trembling fearfully*): No Madame, I haven't done anything.

RÂKIM: How could Janan ever upset me? You shouldn't believe me even if I said such a thing.

JOSEPHINE: I know, and that's how it should be. But there's definitely something wrong with you today.

RÂKIM: Well . . . there is! You know Mr. Ziklas, right? See, his eldest daughter is on her deathbed, and I feel so badly for her. Wouldn't the unexpected and sudden death of a young girl torment a person, Madame? Wouldn't it?

JOSEPHINE: It's lamentable indeed. What's her illness?

RÂKIM: What illness strikes the young? Obviously it's tuberculosis.

JOSEPHINE: Alas, poor girl, alas! I honestly feel sorry for her.

RÂKIM: There is no way you can imagine how sorry I feel. We were practically siblings.

JOSEPHINE: My dear, it isn't necessary to torment yourself as if she were already dead! God willing, nothing will happen to her and she'll recover!

RÂKIM: Right. We consoled her father the same way. Anyway, see, this was one of the reasons for our distress today. The other has to do with Felâtun Bey.

JOSEPHINE: Oh, first we need to know who Felâtun Bey is before we can understand his situation.

RÂKIM: You mean you don't know who Felâtun Bey is?

JOSEPHINE: You've never mentioned him to me.

RÂKIM: I haven't because I didn't see the need. Everyone in Beyoğlu knows who Felâtun Bey is.

JOSEPHINE: Oh, yes, yes, Plato Bey, no?

RÂKIM: Yes, that's him! His name is Felâtun in Turkish and Platon in French.

JOSEPHINE: He went about as the prince of that coquettish actress in Hotel J——. He even pretended to be noble by claiming that his family descended from the Greek god Uranus.

RÂKIM: I don't know if he ever pretended to be noble. But let's say he did. Thank God, we don't have such an institution of bondage in our lands.

JOSEPHINE: So, what is it about this gentleman that makes you feel so sorry for him?

RÂKIM: He lost all of his money, that's what!

JOSEPHINE: Oh, my dear innocent Râkim! Do you have to feel sorry for every fool in this world? Plato Bey isn't a child, is he? Even the children in Beyoğlu figured he'd go through all of his money.

RÂKIM: But I still feel sorry for him Josephine, I do, because at the end of the day he is still my friend.

JOSEPHINE: I don't believe that he's your friend. If he were your friend, he would surely have benefited from your intellect and wisdom. Haven't you heard? Mademoiselle Pauline sent more than fifty thousand francs to her own bank account in France. This is what happens when you live with a mistress who makes you gamble and becomes a party to your money. Whenever there was a pickpocket, she'd introduce him to Plato as a count or a baron and immediately urge him to gamble. Pauline always received a share from the winnings they gained from her lover's losses.

RÂKIM (*listlessly*): Let me tell you something, Josephine. The evil ones from your Europe are more numerous than the good ones!

JOSEPHINE: There's no doubt about that! However, know too, that the foolish ones from your Istanbul are more numerous than the wise ones. From what I've heard, Plato Bey had three or four hundred thousand francs worth of capital. With this capital, he could have lived as a gentleman for three or four hundred thousand years. His father left him all this money. He appointed himself to spend it. Could this gentleman even have earned three or four hundred thousand kuruş on his own?

RÂKIM: If only!

JOSEPHINE: You see? You spend money, yes; however, you spend it only if you can earn it, or even better, after you begin earning it. I say that you should earn money before you spend it because some men assume that they have the capacity and skills to earn money, just as they assume that their fortune will never end. You are young, too. Your capacity and skills have also allowed you to earn but you didn't behave like him, did you?

RÂKIM (*slowly, with a strange smile*): Didn't *you* seduce me?

JOSEPHINE: Oh, what a mama's boy! Look at this baby in his cradle! Oh, I wish that somebody like Mademoiselle (*here, Janan leaves the room after having seen her master whispering in Josephine's ear*) Pauline had gotten a hold on you; I would've loved to see that!

RÂKIM: What could she possibly take from me?

JOSEPHINE: Eventually she would keep you from your work and devastate you! You heartless villain! I've been a mother to you. Well, okay . . . maybe not a mother, but a sister. Or rather, I have been a true friend.

RÂKIM: Don't I know, my dear? I am just joking.

JOSEPHINE: Now you're talking! What's the point of filling your joyful house with grief by worrying about egotistical vagabonds who exercise no self-control? Keep joking. Now give me a sip of that *rakı*. What would the grand ladies think of me if they heard that I was drinking *rakı*? They would think Josephine wicked. Josephine does drink *rakı*; however, she drinks it with Râkım. She did and does love a man but that man is Râkım. And she knows that this won't be announced in Beyoğlu the next day. Oh, my dear, smart Râkım.

Janan, that infidel, took you from my arms but I won't feel resentful towards
the poor girl! If it were anyone else, you would see me take to my bed as well.
By the way, where did Janan go?

RÂKIM: Let's call her. Janan! Janan!

JANAN (*from outside*): What can I do for you, Sir?

The poor girl entered cheerfully when her master called. She offered
drinks to her master and Josephine. Now that Râkım's grief had been dispelled by Josephine's words, he asked for some music. Josephine rose and
rejuvenated everyone with some heartwarming tunes. Afterwards, Janan
sat down in front of the piano, played and sang along. Sometime later that
evening, Josephine said,

JOSEPHINE: Râkım!

RÂKIM: Yes?

JOSEPHINE: Would you accept me as a guest tonight?

RÂKIM (*without hesitation*): By all means, I'd welcome that! I won't only accept it
but I'd also thank you for your sincerity.

JOSEPHINE: But there is one condition.

RÂKIM: Let's hear it.

JOSEPHINE: You won't go to any trouble on my account and you won't give up
your bed. I'll sleep with Janan.

Janan looked happy when she heard that Josephine was going to stay with
them that night and sleep in her bed.

RÂKIM: No, see, that won't happen. Don't you want me to be comfortable? I'll be
very comfortable in my nanny's room. Janan will get up now and change my
bed sheets. Go on, Janan. (*Janan goes cheerfully.*)

JOSEPHINE: I thought we'd agreed to be informal and sincere, no? See, now
you're going to a lot of trouble.

RÂKIM: Not at all!

JOSEPHINE: Besides, why are you changing the sheets?

RÂKIM (*smiling*): In case you feel disgusted.

JOSEPHINE: Now I'll just beat you up! Did we feel disgusted with each other
before? I could've just laid myself down on your bed and smelled your musky
scent tonight.

RÂKIM: Let's leave these jokes aside now and ask Nanny about dinner.

JOSEPHINE: Honestly, this wasn't what I wanted. You've gone to a lot of trouble again.

RÂKIM: My dear, should we starve in order to be informal? There is still time. If we need anything, we can get it right away. Nanny, my dear Nanny!

FEDAYI (*from downstairs*): What do you need, my son?

RÂKIM: Come here for a moment!

JOSEPHINE: Now we will inconvenience Nanny.

RÂKIM: Inconvenience Nanny? How imperfectly you understand this house!

When Fedayi came, Râkım asked her what they were going to eat for dinner that night. Since it was eggplant season, Nanny said that they were going to have a wonderful eggplant kebab, stew, stuffed eggplant, and rice. She added,

FEDAYI: I fear that you're going to detain this madame at our place tonight.

RÂKIM: Yes, we'll have enough food, right?

FEDAYI (*with utmost satisfaction*): Yes, Sir, it'll be enough. Our frying pans are huge. Ask the madame if she desires something else, I'll prepare it right away. We have oil, sugar, and rice . . . thank God we have everything we need.

When Josephine saw Nanny pleased, she realized that even Nanny received her nicely. What's more, when Râkım listed and described the food, Josephine rejoiced like a child and said,

JOSEPHINE: What more could we want? This is already a lot to eat. I'm grateful to her for she likes me!

RÂKIM (*after translating these words to his nanny and telling Josephine what his nanny said in response*): What did you expect, for God's sake? My nanny knows the people that ought to be liked better than I do. Nanny would be happy to have you even if you were to stay for six months.

JOSEPHINE: You are fortunate, Râkım, you are really fortunate. You should kiss the ground and thank God.

RÂKIM: Yes, I am not such an ingrate as to not appreciate how much kindness God shows me. Drowning an orphan like me in such blessings! Giving me dear friends like you.

Janan returned after she was done with her work. Their glasses were all refilled. They passed the time with music and song until dinner. When it was time to set the table, everyone offered to help; Josephine set the table herself, and Râkım went down to get the food, so as not to inconvenience his nanny. They all sat together and ate. If someone were to see them that night, he would assume Josephine was either Râkım's mother or sister, for there was no affectation between them, such that Râkım even asked Josephine to prepare cigarettes for him. This conversation and exchange continued until late at night. Afterwards, they quit the living room, with Josephine retiring to Râkım's bed, Râkım to his nanny's, and Janan to her own room.

There's no question that Josephine interrogated Janan, just as she'd done before.

Bravo, you got it.

And this time Janan confided some of her secrets to her.

Of course! Because their Kağıthane outing, this being Josephine's second time staying overnight, the building up of their friendship over the past three or four months had made the girl that much bolder.

Had it really made her this bold?

So it did! Let us recount it for you to see:

As soon as Janan attended to Josephine and helped her undress, Josephine took it upon herself to interrogate the girl.

JOSEPHINE: Oh, Miss Janan, tell me, doesn't your master love you anymore?

JANAN (*a little embarrassed*): Why shouldn't my master love me? There, you saw it yourself; his resentment today had nothing to do with me.

JOSEPHINE: No, that's not what I'm asking. I mean, does he still love you like a sister?

JANAN (*with a blessed blush inevitably spreading over her face*): He loves me both like a sister and daughter.

JOSEPHINE: Don't blush now, I know how he likes you. I know all about it! But I'd like to hear you say it. That would make me even happier.

JANAN (*overwhelmed*): He loves me in every way.

JOSEPHINE: I said say it!

JANAN: I told you already.

JOSEPHINE: You're not saying it. Have you ever slept together in this room, on this bed?

JANAN (*stricken*): Oh, my dear teacher . . . you are asking me too much.

JOSEPHINE: Yes, I'll ask! I have the right to ask. Am I not like a mother to you?

JANAN: You are, my dear teacher.

JOSEPHINE: Well then, you shouldn't keep any secrets from me, from your mother. Tell me the truth now; did your master make you his concubine?

Upon her teacher's insistence, Janan's intense embarrassment, which we are all acquainted with, reappeared. She wanted to leave Josephine and run away; however, when Josephine restrained her and continued pressuring her, Janan said,

JANAN (*desperately*): He did, my dear teacher.

JOSEPHINE: You're lying!

JANAN: Honest to God, he did. It's been two months now.

JOSEPHINE (*sighing deeply and feeling incredibly pleased*): Bravo Janan, bravo! See, now I'm completely relieved.

JANAN (*slightly more encouraged*): Why, my dear teacher?

JOSEPHINE: It's for me to know.

JANAN: I didn't keep my secret from you, now you shouldn't keep yours from me.

Poor Janan insisted that Josephine also confide her secret to her just as she herself had done. For someone like Josephine could help her overcome many difficulties. After all, she knew all about her master and was Janan's most trusted confidante after Nanny.

JANAN: You're the only one I've told my secret to . . . I haven't even told Nanny.

JOSEPHINE: You mean Nanny hasn't figured it out yet?

JANAN: No, my dear teacher, I haven't told her.

JOSEPHINE: Why not? Are you afraid of her?

JANAN: No!

JOSEPHINE: Well then, if you're not afraid, why don't you tell her?

JANAN: If I told her, Nanny would also be happy, but . . .

JOSEPHINE: In that case, why not tell her?

JANAN: Oh, how can say it? I'm embarrassed!

The poor girl said, "I'm embarrassed" with such bashfulness, which another girl would've said with excessive pride, that Josephine's sincere love for Janan, who was too embarrassed to tell her secret even to Nanny, multiplied. In recognition of the trust the girl showed her, Josephine said,

JOSEPHINE: Yes, I'm relieved. I'm relieved because no matter how smart and mature a young man Râkım is, since he wasn't involved with anyone, I was afraid that if he set his heart on someone who could ruin him, then you and Nanny would be ruined along with him. See, he just told me tonight that a young man like him was ruined after losing a fortune of hundreds of thousands of francs. It's true that Râkım has loved you since he bought you. Indeed, as you said, he loved you like a sister. Yet, sisterly love doesn't settle one's heart. The heart still looks for a place to settle. See, it has now settled on you. I am confident that Râkım won't even glance at anyone else from now on. You should be confident, too.

JANAN: My dear teacher! Can I ask you something?

JOSEPHINE (*sincerely*): Go ahead, my dear.

JANAN: You know those girls our master is tutoring, don't you?

JOSEPHINE: Yes, the eldest is dispirited and at death's door.

JANAN: That's what I was going to ask you about! Master thinks about that girl so much.

JOSEPHINE: And you're really worried about this, is that right?

JANAN: It's not so much what I think; I just don't want Master to dwell on it so much.

JOSEPHINE: Don't act like a child, didn't I tell you just now? If your master acted this way before making you his concubine, then you'd be right to worry about it. From now on, however, even if a houri comes down from heaven, nothing will happen. I know Râkım Efendi much better than you do!

JANAN (*embracing and kissing Josephine*): Oh, my dear teacher! You've brought peace to my heart.

JOSEPHINE (*also kissing the girl*): Look at this courtesan here! When did you acquire Râkım that you started feeling jealous? You naughty little girl!

There, the secrets that Janan revealed to Josephine that night are clear from this conversation and since Nanny still didn't know about them, they can certainly be considered secrets.

After the aforementioned conversation, Josephine went to bed and Janan retired to her room. However, she didn't find it empty or vacant. Râkım, who had been waiting for her for the last half hour, had nearly caught the entire conversation between Janan and Josephine.

When the girl saw her master, she quickly realized that he must have heard the secret conversation she'd had with Josephine, and turned pale with fear. However, after seeing no sign on Râkım's face to warrant such fear, and observing that his mournful mood from that morning had vanished, she felt relieved and made no sound when her master placed his finger on her mouth to order her to be silent.

Then another whispered conversation began in Janan's room. Since there was only a flimsy wall between Josephine and them, it wasn't possible for them to speak loudly. However, had Josephine attempted to listen in on their whispered conversation, she would've heard nothing but a confirmation of the assurance she'd given Janan. Why should we write needlessly about that assurance again here? It would be enough simply to convey the words uttered by Râkım. "Nanny went to sleep! I couldn't get to sleep, and so I came here, Janan!"

After fifteen or twenty minutes, these whispers also ended, and a general silence indicated that everybody in the house had fallen into a sweet sleep.

As it was summer, Janan, as she had been instructed to do, woke her master, oh no, her *dear* master, early in the morning, and although we say "early," it was nearly dawn. He got up and went to Nanny's room, which was still covered in darkness, to move his bed there without her noticing but he saw that Nanny was not in bed. He heard her rattling the pots and pans downstairs. Thinking, "You see, Nanny also knows what's going on now. It's all right though, wasn't this what she hoped for all along? Let her rejoice," he entered his bed innocently daydreaming and went back to sleep.

Two hours later, Râkım woke up again and found everyone up. Since the joy of morning is most special in winter, Josephine didn't find it as enjoyable to look out at the garden on that summer morning. Nevertheless, they amused themselves for another hour, and then Josephine got up and got dressed. After saying goodbye to Râkım, she left the house and went off to work.

Hadn't Râkım said something like "Let Nanny rejoice," when he'd moved his things into her room that morning? Would you be surprised if we told you that he observed the opposite of what he had expected? Nanny had such an expression, such a look on her face . . . God forbid! In fact, when Râkım asked if she had any major purchases to make from the market that day, she said that they didn't need anything; every single letter of her response, however, hit Râkım on the head like a stone.

Oh, our dear Nanny! As if it were the end of the world!

Yes, see, our nanny, who loved Râkım like her own son and Janan like her own daughter and deemed it the greatest honor to marry them off, was full of rage and anger!

After Râkım departed, Janan came up to Nanny and told her with gratitude and contentment that she was very pleased that Josephine had come and fended off all of her master's grief. She said, if it hadn't been for that good, sweet woman, her master would have remained in the doldrums.

FEDAYI (*about to cry out of sadness and rage*): If that woman enters this house one more time . . . she can fend off your master's grief all she wants!

JANAN: What's wrong, Nanny?

FEDAYI: I know what happened. Poor girl! I know what happened.

JANAN (*fearfully*): My dear Nanny, what happened for God's sake? I really want to know.

FEDAYI: If you knew what happened, you'd also never want to let that woman in this house, and make Master swear that he will never see her again.

JANAN: Do I ever disagree with you, my dear Nanny? But tell me what happened, for God's sake, dear Nanny! What is it that made you so angry?

FEDAYI: It's not good to share such things with you but since I am so bothered about it, I won't be able to keep it from you anymore, so here, I'll tell you.

JANAN: Say it, dear Nanny. Just say it, for God's sake!

FEDAYI: What I want to tell you is . . . What would you say if I told you that Master escaped from his bed, thinking I was asleep?

JANAN (*blushing*): What?

FEDAYI: Don't you get it?

JANAN: I don't understand, dear Nanny.

FEDAYI: You silly girl! You don't realize what's going on. So this was why we couldn't make Master fancy you. Last night, he left my room and went directly to that French madame's room. I heard it all the way from down here in the kitchen, when he slowly crept back this morning. How can I consent to this happening?

Suspicions such as these would probably cause any other girl to give a mocking smile but for Janan, it only made her more hesitant and embarrassed. However, she couldn't let her Nanny feel such anger toward her master out of groundless and evil suppositions, fearing that something bad might happen if these misunderstandings led Nanny to utter some harsh words toward the already sorrowful Râkım.

JANAN: Well, dear Nanny, can I tell you something?

FEDAYI: Let's hear it.

JANAN: I wouldn't expect that from either Josephine or my master.

FEDAYI: You must be joking! I told you, you have no idea what's going on around you.

JANAN: But I do, Nanny, I do.

FEDAYI (*her suspicions vanishing immediately after seeing Janan blush*): Girl! You can't be serious!

JANAN (*lowering her face*): Yes, Nanny, I am.

FEDAYI: Was he with you?

JANAN (*seeing no need for more embarrassment, runs to Nanny, embraces and kisses her*): Am I not your daughter, dear Nanny? Are you not my mother, eh?

FEDAYI (*with a greater happiness than Janan's, kissing her*): So, that's it? Oh, yes, you were my daughter, but now even more so. Oh, thank God! Poor madame, poor Râkım, I accused them both wrongly for no reason. Of course I give you my blessings!

This loyal Arab's rage and anger from a moment ago turned into pleasure and joy of the same magnitude and she gave Janan a slew of instructions. Especially after Janan told Nanny about what a loyal, loving and friendly woman Josephine has been to both her master and herself, the Arab's former affection for Josephine increased.

When Râkım returned home that night, Fedayi couldn't hide her pleasure and broached the subject with him. Râkım admitted and even said with pride that he hadn't taken Janan as a concubine but had married her. He added that they were going to marry legally. Imagine Nanny's joy! Both Râkım and Janan were in her arms. She kissed them both.

When Josephine came for the next lesson, Nanny used Janan as a translator to explain the situation to Josephine and asked for forgiveness for her mistake, thinking, "I shall not be burdened with this sin." Josephine burst out laughing, which expressed many things, and she said, "If Râkım and Janan have a friend more loyal than I, it's you. I know that you hoped to see Janan and Râkım's marriage and made a lot of effort to make this happen. However, you only encouraged Janan. I undertook to encourage Râkım. If you don't believe me, ask him. He's a trustworthy young man; he won't deny it." In fact, when the evening came and Râkım arrived, he didn't deny how much Josephine had encouraged his love for Janan and gratefully said that if Nanny were one of the two people who loved him in this world, Josephine would be the other.

Chapter 11

JAN'S ILLNESS intensified after Monsieur Z——, Râkım, and her father failed in the game they'd attempted to play out in front of her and after she'd revealed her secret. Because of this, Mr. Ziklas was worried about his other daughter, Margaret, and whisked her off to Alexandria with some ruses and promises. Upon the girl's request, Mr. Ziklas invited Râkım by letter, asking to see her off at the ferry.

Râkım got on a boat with Margaret and her parents by the shore at the Kurşunlu Mahzen area and headed out to the ferry. The captain respectfully offered them tea and coffee in the first-class cabin, as Mr. Ziklas had entrusted his daughter to his care. After sitting for a while, they got ready to depart, and while Margaret took leave from her parents, she slowly whispered into Râkım's ear in Turkish, "Oh, Râkım! If it were possible to divide you into three pieces, I would do everything I could to own one of them. I had to give up when I found out about my sister's interest in you. If I hadn't learned about it, you would have seen me confined to my bed, too! I did what I could; I hardened my heart like a stone and saved myself from the claws of death, which is your love. Send my greetings to Janan. Let her know that she is the murderer of my sister. But assure her that she is not to blame for this murder."

How peculiar!

Yes, this part is a bit peculiar. Do you want to hear something more peculiar? Felâtun Bey, who was assuming the position of district governor of a Mediterranean island, was on the very same ferry leaving from Istanbul. Râkım ran into him on the deck.

RÂKIM: Well hello, Sir! God bless you.

FELÂTUN: I am leaving the pleasures of Istanbul to you, Brother. I've been appointed as a district governor for the —— Island, I'm leaving. Now you can fully enjoy yourself with Mademoiselle Ziklas.

RÂKIM (*sighing heavily*): We're going to take one of them to her grave one of these days. The other one is going to Alexandria on this same ferry. If anybody is enjoying the pleasures of Istanbul, it's you.

FELÂTUN (*sighing more heavily than Râkım Efendi*): Yes, you're right. After spending all that was left from my father, I borrowed around 150,000 kuruş. Not bad for pleasure, eh?

RÂKIM: It's all right, my friend. It takes time for people to come to their senses. You won't do it again.

FELÂTUN: With the salary I'll receive, even if I live long enough to feed myself and pay off my debt of 150,000 kuruş with what remains, I'll only be able to find time for pleasure again in my nineties.

RÂKIM: Oh come on, my friend, aren't all debts payable?

FELÂTUN: No, my friend! I indulged myself in pleasure, acted like a child, and made every possible mistake. Trust me when I tell you that that I'll be content with my salary and work honestly and candidly where I am appointed as an official.

RÂKIM: God knows I've always trusted you. May God promptly bring you success. What I mean to say is that I hope you work your way up, pay off your debts, and find the opportunity to enjoy yourself with your earnings.

FELÂTUN: As long as one serves loyally, there's no reason for it not to happen.

RÂKIM: See, that's the kind of attitude I'd like you to adopt as you assume your official duties. God will be with you if you believe this and commit to it. I wish you every success, brother! You won't forget us, will you? Let's write to each other every now and then.

FELÂTUN: Certainly, *adieu mon cher!*

RÂKIM: *Bon voyage, mon ami!*

What happened to the English family's grudge? The animosity between the Ziklas family and Felâtun, which had developed as a result of the mayonnaise incident, continued in all its intensity. Although they saw Felâtun bidding farewell to Râkım, they didn't even greet him. But weren't they justified?

They got back on the boat, which they had taken there, and went back to the shore near the Kurşunlu Mahzen area. Râkım told them that he had some work to take care of and returned to his house. Mr. Ziklas and his wife busied themselves with desperate Jan, who was confined to her bed. Since the doctor stopped occupying himself with the poor girl, her parents gave her everything she asked for while they waited for her imminent demise. That day, the girl felt like eating meat. She called the cook and ordered some good meat broth and instructed him to make it very strong. Her parents found her eating the soup and breaking biscuits into it. Since they hadn't witnessed anything like it for a long time, they were surprised. After eating her food, she didn't lie down in bed but sat up and asked them to call Doctor Monsieur Z——.

The doctor arrived an hour later. The girl informed him that she felt some sort of itching on her chest, something that she'd never felt before.

DOCTOR: Are you still bleeding?

JAN: Not for the last two days.

DOCTOR: Any phlegm?

JAN: Two days ago, I was spitting up bloody phlegm.

DOCTOR: Very well, very well, so you're feeling more at ease. Now that you are at ease, it isn't necessary to make any new arrangements. You should eat well and protect yourself from the cold.

Even though the doctor gave these orders, his heart was actually saying, "This means that two days from now, you'll be completely and finally at ease, for the symptoms of this illness disappear in the last days of a person's life." However, how could the parents know what the doctor's heart was saying? When the doctor said, "All right, all right," they assumed that their girl was really all right.

But what does this illness do really? It makes more room in one's stomach, is this what it does? Jan's stomach suddenly became so strong. Since the concentrated meat broth was improving her lungs, her cough went away altogether and they forgot about her blood and phlegm. The strange thing is that not two but five days went by after the doctor's visit and she hadn't died! Moreover, it was starting to seem as if she didn't want to either.

Accordingly, they called the doctor again who, after examining the girl thoroughly, couldn't make sense of how the illness had taken such a turn. As a precaution, before he departed the doctor gave her a syrup that would neither benefit nor harm her, suggested she continue to eat well, and protect herself from the cold, moisture, and dust.

How effective the doctor's medicine was this time! The girl's stomach was gradually getting stronger. They called the doctor on the second day as well and asked for the same medicine; only this time they asked for a slightly stronger version of it. The man knew that it couldn't have such an effect but he didn't want to spoil the good impression his medicine created and prepared a supposedly stronger one.

Yes, this time the medicine had a stronger effect! The patient who could barely move in her bed started wandering around the room. Now, can you refute what Molière said about doctors? The most scientific aspect of being a doctor is understanding if a patient is dead; otherwise even if they can diagnose the specific disease, since diseases have many types, they can never discern its type. The books on pathology say there is no medicine for tuberculosis and all the medicines that are being prescribed are experimental. In fine print, however, the last two lines warn, "There are people who survive this illness on their own." Now, when our Doctor Z—— saw that Jan was returning to life, he thought, "So this last remark in the pathology book is true!" Feeling surprised and after observing that the girl would definitely recover, he pranced around like Luqman the Wise. "If my mother-in-law were with me now, even she would pass herself off as Hippocrates," he thought to himself.

Seriously! The girl really came back to herself. She even left the sickbed for good. She put on her morning dress. Although Mr. Ziklas wrote to Râkım every two days about the changes in the girl's condition, he always added, "There, my son, I've given you all there is to know. However, if you come and visit my daughter, I fear that her illness might return."

Meanwhile, what would you say if we told you that the girl asked for her teacher when she regained her health and began getting bored? Before Doctor Z—— could object, her father objected, saying that it might cause her illness to return, but it was impossible to convince the girl who assured them that she couldn't feel anything like love for Râkım in her heart anymore. She even consented when her father suggested that she get married to her cousin from Izmir, who was already eager to marry her. With these assurances, a servant was sent to fetch Râkım.

When Râkım saw the girl alive, he was delirious with happiness. When Jan saw Râkım, she felt greater peace and tranquility, and recited the couplet, "If all the horizons gather around your head, it is not possible that desire for you be driven from my head." Râkım told her that these were the very couplets that had put her in this condition in the first place, and asked her not to place importance on such poetic dreams. The girl assured him that she was going to make an effort to protect the life she had regained, and with this, everybody rejoiced.

Râkım was so happy that he choked up but Jan and her parents understood what it was that he wanted to say. Nevertheless, after Jan asked him what he was trying to say, Râkım replied, "Miss, what I'm going to say is for Monsieur Ziklas!" and pulled him aside. "Do you see, Monsieur Ziklas? God Most Gracious returned to you your saintly daughter and 300,000 liras of fortune." When Mr. Ziklas heard the contented, trustworthy and loyal Râkım utter these words, his love for him deepened and he genuinely wanted to embrace him.

We'll take no delight in getting wordy from now on. Let's be brief and settle this amicably:

Nearly three months had passed since Mr. Ziklas wrote what he needed to write and completed the necessary correspondence when Margaret returned from Alexandria, Jan's fiancé arrived from Izmir, and one of Ziklas's nephews, whose marriage to Margaret was decided upon incidentally, came from Aleppo, and at the ball organized for the girls' weddings in November, Râkım danced the polka for the first time in his life.

What's more, when he returned home the next day, his nanny informed him that a new life was playing around in Janan's belly; hearing this news made Râkım happier than anything else.

And so we proudly inform our readers that six months later Râkım delighted his loyal friend Josephine by putting a swaddled cherubic baby boy on her lap; and with this, we bring our story to an end.

THE END

Afterword

*

Index

Afterword

A. HOLLY SHISSLER

FELÂTUN BEY AND RÂKIM EFENDI (1875) is one of the earliest examples of the Ottoman novel. Ahmet Midhat was called in his own day the People's First Teacher (a label drawn from the title of some textbooks he wrote early in his career) due to his prolific writing and commitment to educating a broad public. Humorous and moralizing at the same time, *Felâtun Bey and Râkım Efendi* struck a chord with a wide audience such that its characters, particularly Felâtun, constitute enduring types that frequently populate subsequent Turkish literature. "The Felatun type is the first example in the Turkish novel of the *alafranga* dandy [*züppe*] who later reappeared in such works as Recaizade [Ekrems]'s *The Love of Carriages* (1896), Hüseyin Rahmi's *Always in Love* (1911), and Ömer Seyfettin's *Efruz Bey* (1919)."[1]

Ahmet Midhat did not invent this type, which had earlier made its appearance in genres such as stage plays and caricatures, but his drawing of it in *Felâtun Bey and Râkım Efendi* is so vivid that it has served as its quintessential expression in Turkish letters until today. In this sense it might be compared with Turgenev's *Diary of a Superfluous Man*. Turgenev did not invent the type of the "Superfluous Man," which was seen as symptomatic of a pervasive and much deeper social problem. But his work embodied this type so successfully that the "Superfluous Man" became a byword for this character type and the social ills associated with it. Indeed, what

1. *Türk Edebiyatı Ansiklopedisi* (Istanbul: Cem Yayınevi, n.d.), 495.

modern critics say about the figure of the "Superfluous Man" in the world of Russian literature could easily be applied to Ahmet Midhat's *alafranga* dandy—namely, that he makes his appearance soon after the encounter with Western European letters and that he appears "not just as another literary type, but as a paradigm of a person who has lost a point, a place, and a presence in life: the superfluous man is the homeless man."[2]

Felâtun Bey and Râkım Efendi is a moralizing tale that juxtaposes the two eponymous characters. The storyline of the "Tale of Sir Plato and Mr. Number the Scribe," as the title may be somewhat freely translated, makes it abundantly clear to the reader which character's life and path are preferable, both from the point of view of the satisfaction of the men living it, and from the point of view of the good of wider society. Râkım's thrift and hard work are rewarded, while Felâtun's dissolute, pointless lifestyle also leads him to his just desserts—penury and an absence of meaningful relationships. The contrasts are emphasized at every turn in the story: Râkım comes from a very modest background and has grown up in poverty while Felâtun is the pampered only son of a wealthy father; Râkım works hard to get himself educated while Felâtun has had a fancy education handed to him on a platter; Râkım drums up employment opportunities for himself in government offices, but also outside of them, and he works hard at his jobs, while Felâtun lives off a government sinecure procured through family connections and rarely shows up at the office. The negative side of these contrasts is embodied by Felâtun who is, in addition to being aimless and dissolute, a slave to European fashion. Indeed, European fashion is the marker for all his shortcomings. Thus *Felâtun Bey and Râkım Efendi* captures one of the great concerns of the age—namely, that the answer given during the Tanzimat reform era to the question "What should we do to save the Ottoman state and society?" had turned out to be a kind of uncritical and indeed superficial adoption of European modes of life that, so far from leading to the strengthening of Ottoman society and state, had further undermined it. But while the book represents a set of sharply drawn contrasts, these are not contrasts

2. David Patterson, *Exile* (Lexington: University Press of Kentucky, 1995), 2.

between old and new, European and Ottoman. Rather both men represent something new: a very modern evil, personified as the pointless Europeanized dandy—Felâtun, and a modern alternative—Râkım. Salvation, the book suggests, was not to be sought in a return to "traditional" usages. Râkım is not a "traditional" Ottoman nor yet one who rejects European innovations per se. He is educated in both Ottoman and European subjects and makes his living from both providing translations from French as well as lessons in Ottoman. He is worldly and frequents the salons and clubs of Beyoğlu in moderation; he is comfortable in both Ottoman and European-style social situations in terms of food, drink, clothing, and manners. But he is profoundly different from Felâtun in that he has both ambition and discipline. We see throughout the novel his work ethic and commitment to planning. He is, in this sense, the model of the modern man so often discussed and longingly anticipated by Ottoman reformers, the educated Ottoman with a sense of "sa'y ve emel" or "striving and purpose," a figure whose advent in society was broadly understood to be the necessary ingredient for Ottoman progress. A vexing question in this formulation, however, was how to produce such men, and Felâtun Bey and Râkım Efendi offers us not merely contrasting portrayals of successful and abortive modernization, it also implicitly offers us Ahmet Midhat's account of what leads to success or failure in this endeavor.

Râkım's work ethic and self-discipline initially seem to have their roots in necessity (he starts life as a man in somewhat straitened circumstances, with his widowed mother and her devoted slave Fedayi taking in sewing to support him), but it becomes something that has its roots in his sense of responsibility—first to the aging Fedayi, later to his young female slave, Janan. Ahmet Midhat emphasizes that Râkım needs this sense of responsibility and attachment both to keep him going and to give him a moral compass. Here we are not talking about responsibility of just any kind. Rather, we are talking about responsibility born of love as well as duty, responsibility that is therefore not a burden, but a source of happiness, something that grounds Râkım and propels him forward.

This sense of responsibility is revealed most forcefully through the evolution of his feelings for Janan. Râkım has already attained a certain level of material success and stability when he acquires her, and therefore is potentially in some danger of losing his way. However, the transformation of Janan, through his generosity, from slave girl to an increasingly assured, educated, and knowledgeable young woman, engages his emotions in a new way and ultimately keeps him on the right path. For this to be possible, Janan must be a woman who can be a true partner in his labors. The novel requires that she must be a proper companion to Râkım in the sense of being well suited to him in age, attractiveness, and intelligence, but she must also become educated, aware of the wider world, and able to freely choose to join her life to his. Her decision in favor of a life in a modest middle-class home, largely segregated from society, rather than pursuing a possible "career" as concubine (*cariye*) in a great and wealthy household where she could have lived a life of privilege and influence, is the moment that marks her out definitively as a possible partner for Râkım and mother to his child. It is from and in such a nest, the book assures us, that men such as Râkım spring and reproduce themselves.

Companionate marriage, as opposed to marriage as a business contract between families, was an idea that had gained wide currency in the nineteenth-century Middle East as not merely a marker of modernity, but as a generative element that was essential to helping construct a modern society. In this respect, the story of Râkım is an early literary endorsement of a new social norm. However, what is surprising, as Robert Finn has noted, is the fact that the young woman in question in this novel is a slave (until the very end of the book) and her slave status is not a problem that lies at the crux of the novel, as was typical of other fictions of the period. This very unusual—indeed, distressing—aspect of the novel is not its only unusual feature.

The other striking and quite uncommon feature of this novel is that Ahmet Midhat doesn't merely lampoon Felâtun. He also offers up the alternative in Râkım, and suggests that what makes Râkım the perfect counterpoise is his ability to be a modern Ottoman, not a fake European. He is educated and entrepreneurial, but his intimate life is lived in the Ottoman way, in an Ottoman Muslim quarter of the city. The food he eats, the people who inhabit his home, the way he manages his domestic arrangements, are all Ottoman rather than European.

At the same time, at the heart of it all is the genuine love between two people who are or become genuine equals in human (rather than formal or institutional) terms. By choosing to illustrate this point using a slave girl who is happy in her condition, Ahmet Midhat is making a very strong statement. He is rejecting what seems to him an excessive and immoral individualism in European social arrangements, which he comments on forcefully in his account of his European tour, *Avrupa'da bir Cevelan* (A Tour in Europe) and elsewhere. He makes the point that the bonds of love are *just that*—in other words, that they are both bonds and are based on love. The book suggests that a healthy society has at its core families in which people *choose* to be responsible for each other (and in that sense choose not to be perfectly free as individuals), where its members find pleasure in not putting themselves first. These are the families that produce and sustain productive, engaged citizens. The trappings of modernity grafted onto the scion of a traditional "patrimonial" family like that of Mustafa Meraki Efendi, Felâtun's father, offer society only the Ottoman version of the "Superfluous Man": Felâtun Bey.

The choice of a slave girl to illustrate this dichotomy was obviously a conscious one on the part of Ahmet Midhat, certainly intended as pointed, and perhaps even intended as shocking. While Ahmet Midhat placed great value on freedom in the sense of an individual's ability to make (informed) choices, he strongly opposed what he saw as an excessive and morally corrosive individualism in European societies—that is, a system of values in which it appeared to him that individuals considered only their own desires and well-being without regard for others or for society more broadly. Furthermore, though Ahmet Midhat was an advocate of greater education and inclusion in some aspects of the public sphere for women, as can be seen from his support for Fatma Aliye, one of the first female Ottoman novelists, he rejected the notion of equality in the sense of formal sameness. The sexual division of labor and social roles, with men freely assuming economic and protective responsibilities toward women, who in all important ways were their physical and intellectual companions and who had freely chosen them, was, according to Ahmet Midhat, the cornerstone of a healthy, "go-ahead" society. In this sense we may also take the novel as a response to European comments on the "woman question" and European criticisms of sex segregation in Ottoman society. Just as Felâtun is the anti-Râkım, Madame Polini is the anti-Janan, and Ahmet Midhat invites us to consider which of them is really free and happy. He does so in 1875, when the Ottoman Empire was already in the process of suppressing the slave trade and there was broad awareness of international, especially British, opprobrium around the institution of slavery. Ehud Toledano has noted that this international criticism led to a certain defensiveness among Ottoman thinkers, who tended to condemn slavery but nevertheless emphasized what they saw as the gentler nature of Ottoman/Islamic slavery. However, Ahmet Midhat had already expressed himself forcefully on the negative consequences of slavery in one of his earliest novellas, entitled *Slavery* (*Esaret*), in 1870. Thus one must see his choice of a slave to fill the role of the anti-Madame Polini not as an apology for Ottoman slavery, but as a rhetorical device.[3]

3. Ehud Toledano has discussed this apologetic attitude toward Ottoman/Islamic slavery by the Ottomans themselves and by some later commentators in his impressive *As if Silent and Absent: Bonds of Enslavement in the Islamic Middle East* (New Haven, CT: Yale Univ. Press, 2007), 15–23. The slave trade in the Ottoman Empire was suppressed through a gradual and complex process in the nineteenth century. Thus, slave trade in the Persian Gulf was banned in 1847, the African slave trade was prohibited in 1857, and the Anglo-Ottoman convention for the suppression of the slave trade was signed in 1880. However, the case of Circassians fell outside these acts. Somewhere from a half a million to a million Circassians fled Russia for the Ottoman Empire at mid-century. A certain number of these belonged to an enserfed or enslaved caste, property of their higher caste brethren. The question of their status was a complex policy problem for Ottoman statesmen. Moreover, Circassian and Transcaucasian women continued to be prized additions to Ottoman harems. Finally, suppression of the slave trade was not the same thing as the abolition of slavery. Slavery, especially household slavery of women, continued to exist in the Ottoman Empire, albeit on a reduced scale, right into the twentieth century. The question of slavery and suppression of the slave trade in the Ottoman Empire has been treated in a number of works, among which we may mention, in addition to the work cited above, the following: Hakan Erdem, *Slavery in the Ottoman Empire and its Demise* (New York: St. Martin's Press, 1996); Ehud Toledano, *Slavery and Abolition in the Ottoman Middle East* (Seattle: Univ. of Washington Press, 1998) and *The Ottoman Slave Trade and its Suppression, 1840–1890* (Princeton, NJ: Princeton Univ. Press, 1982); and Madeline Zilfi, *Women and Slavery in the Late Ottoman Empire: The Design of Difference* (New York: Cambridge Univ. Press, 2010).

Râkım's life in many ways mirrors that of his creator, Ahmet Midhat, a fact that has been noted by Turkish critics. Ahmet Midhat was born to a family of very modest means in the Tophane district of Istanbul in 1844. His father was a small-time cloth merchant and his mother (a refugee from Russian Transcaucasia) took in sewing to supplement the family's income. Ahmet Midhat spent his childhood years as a shop assistant in Istanbul's Egyptian Bazaar.[4] He later recalled the long hours, hard work, poor food, inadequate clothing, and many beatings he endured during this period. However, he learned the ins and outs of running a shop, began to earn tips while serving in the shop, and persuaded a neighboring shop-keeper to teach him to read and write in the evenings. He began to earn extra income by writing letters for other people in his spare time. Upon the death of his father, his older brother, who was part of the network of the great nineteenth-century Ottoman statesman and reformer, Midhat Pasha, moved the family to Vidin, where the young Ahmet enrolled in school. Later he moved with his brother to Niş, where he completed his education at one of the new reformed middle schools (rüşdiye) established throughout the Ottoman Empire in the nineteenth century. His academic success was noted at the time by Midhat Pasha, who was in the habit of keeping track of the progress of the school's students. When Midhat Pasha became governor of the newly created Danubian province (Tuna Vilayeti), Ahmet was called to its capital city, Rusçuk (modern Ruse, in Bulgaria), to take a position in Pasha's scribal service. At this time Midhat Pasha, impressed with Ahmet Midhat's energy and ability, gave him his own name "Midhat," as a sign of favor (hence the name Ahmet Midhat), and made arrangements for him to learn French. He also encouraged him to pursue classical Ottoman learning at the local medrese. During these years, among other activities, Ahmet Midhat did some writing and translating

---

4. There are a number of publications that give accounts of Ahmet Midhat Efendi's life. Among the most detailed, to which the present account is indebted, are the following: Mustafa Nihat Özön, Türkçede Roman Hakkında bir Deneme (Istanbul: Remzi Kitabevi, n.d.), and İhsan Sungu, "Ahmet Midhat Efendi'nin Hayatı Üzerine," in İdeal Gazeteci Efendi Babamız Ahmet Midhat, ed. Münir Süleyman Çapanoğlu (Istanbul: Gazeteci Cemiyeti Yayınları, 1964).

for the newly established provincial gazette. Never one to lose an opportunity, he used this connection to teach himself all the technical aspects of printing and lithography as well. These years were the time of wild youth for Ahmet Midhat, who developed spendthrift habits and rakish behavior. His family arranged his marriage in hopes that this would settle him, but when this expedient failed to produce the desired result, his older brother cut him off, throwing him out of the family home and obliging him to make his way entirely on his own. In 1869, when Midhat Pasha was appointed governor of another newly established Ottoman administrative unit, the province of Baghdad, he charged Ahmet Midhat with establishing a publishing house there and producing the new province's official gazette. Ahmet Midhat traveled to Baghdad as part of Pasha's initial 104-person team, and soon began to bring out *Zevra* (*Baghdad*), the official paper (and the region's first). During this period he also began to write and print *First Teacher* (*Hace-i Evvel*), a kind of textbook for the new technical and trade school that Midhat Pasha was setting up in Baghdad (and that was later established in all provinces as part of the Empire-wide provincial reforms).

While he was in Baghdad province, his older brother, who was occupying a post in Basra, died, leaving Ahmet Midhat the head of a numerous family. Lacking better alternatives, he sent the family back to Istanbul. When, shortly thereafter, it was announced that the government was holding a competition for new textbooks to be used in the Empire's elementary schools, Ahmet Midhat submitted a copy of *Hace-i Evvel*, resigned his post with Midhat Pasha, and returned to Istanbul in 1871. However, his text was not adopted. Thus Ahmet Midhat entered into a period when he was hard pressed to support himself and his family, but during which he gained an enormous amount of publishing experience. Through personal connections he was offered the position of editor-in-chief of the weekly journal the *Military Register* (*Ceride-i Askeriye*). At the same time, he set up a small printing press inside his own home and began to print and distribute *First Teacher* in installments. Similarly, he published a series of short stories and translations that he had begun writing in Baghdad. He gave this series a title, *Letâif-i Rivâyat* (Amusing Tales) and continued publishing works in this series until 1894. This was a shoestring operation: Ahmet Midhat did all the technical aspects of the printing himself, and used the women and children of the household to perform the rest of the labor. He then distributed these publications with the help of water sellers, tobacconists, and peddlers who sold them throughout the city. But there was not initially a great audience for such works, and the family was falling on very hard times. Fortunately he was offered the opportunity to do some writing for *Basiret Gazetesi* (Discernment), and the earnings from this together with the salary from the *Military Register* allowed him to get by. He moved his press to a commercial location, and with time made it into more of a going concern by taking on paid printing jobs, as well as continuing to publish his own work. Throughout this period he generally expanded his connections in the literary and journalistic world and undertook a number of writing and publishing projects. It was at this time that he came into contact with members of the liberal-minded and constitutionalist Ottoman intellectual opposition known as the Young Ottomans. He began writing some unsigned pieces for their journals. Partly due to his association with them and partly due to the publication of an essay in 1872 that defended materialism, *"Duvardan Bir Seda"* (A Voice from Behind the Wall), he was sent into internal banishment on Rhodes in the spring of 1873 at the same time as many others of the Young Ottoman group. Ahmet Midhat was not idle during this time. He founded a school on the island together with friend and fellow political exile Ebüzziya Tevfik, and he also wrote a number of novels which were sent to Istanbul and published under his own name by the Kırk Anbar Press, with his friend Mehmet Cevdet, who held the press's license, taking responsibility for them. *Felâtun Bey and Râkım Efendi* was among these, appearing in 1875.

In 1876, due to a general amnesty following the toppling of Sultan Abdülaziz, Ahmet Midhat was able to return to Istanbul. He developed good relations with the regime of Sultan Abdülhamid II, who came to the throne as a liberal sultan willing to accept the proclamation of a constitution in 1876, but who by 1878 had dismissed the parliament and embarked on what was to be a long and authoritarian reign lasting until 1909. This positive relationship with the throne meant that for the rest of his life Ahmet Midhat held a number of official posts. Among these were editor of the official state gazette, *Takvim-i Vekayi* (The Calendar of Events), and directorship of the imperial press, the *Matbaa-i Amire*, as well as various posts on the Committee for Public Health. In addition, he was sent as the official Ottoman representative to the International Congress of Orientalists in Stockholm in 1889.

Among his most important achievements was the founding of the longest running Istanbul Ottoman daily paper, *Tercüman-i Hakikat* (The Interpreter of Truth), which appeared virtually uninterrupted from 1878 to 1922. He actively managed and edited the paper until his retirement in 1909. Here, in addition to news items, editorials, shipping information, etc., he published many fictions in serial form, both his own and those of promising new authors, many of whom, like Hüseyin Rahmi Gürpınar and Ahmet Rasim, became important figures in the world of Ottoman and Turkish literature. In addition to his many efforts as a novelist and journalist, he published a number of important works in other fields including economics and religion. His translations included not only novels and short stories, but also works of philosophy.

After his retirement from publishing in 1909 (that is, after the Young Turk revolution that would eventually sweep Abdülhamid II from power), he taught a number of general courses on history, religion, and philosophy at the Darülfunun (later Istanbul University) as well as a pedagogy course at the Darülmuallimat (Istanbul Normal School) until his death in 1912.

Though he held a variety of public posts throughout his adult life, he was quite unlike many littérateurs of his day, who were men of means publishing in order to express their views; Ahmet Midhat always combined his sense of mission as a publisher and author with a concern for making a living from those activities. The volume and scope of his publications (more than 200) and activities (also considerable) was prodigious; he was intensely interested in both learning and disseminating knowledge on a wide array of topics. The beneficiary of formal education in both "traditional" Ottoman and "modern" subjects, he was later able to write widely on a variety of matters and to translate works from French. As an author and publisher, he worked so hard and wrote so copiously that he labeled himself a writing machine and his contemporaries agreed. Among the many topics he took an interest in was language reform, and he was a champion of simplifying the Ottoman literary language and style in a way that would make the world of letters more available to more people. This is visible in novels like *Felâtun Bey and Râkim Efendi.* While descriptive sections of the novel retain a more ornamental style with relatively heavier use of Persian and Arabic-based vocabulary and structures, the sections where there is dialogue or where the author is directly addressing the reader employ a language patterned on the natural speech of ordinary people. As late as 1964, thirty years into the Turkish Republic's radical reform of modern Turkish, Niyazi Berkes could observe "His [Ahmet Midhat's] Turkish is comprehensible to a high school boy even today."[5] But beyond the question of language, the style also helped make the work accessible. The deep vein of humor that permeates the novel prevents it from becoming a turgid morality tale. Incidents such as the mayonnaise episode at the Ziklas's luncheon leaven the narrative, and the author's commentary is characterized by an ironically humorous tone.

Among his many nonfiction publications, Ahmet Midhat wrote two works on recent history at the behest of Sultan Abdülhamid II: *Üss-ü İnkilap* (Basis of Reform) (1877–78), and *Zübdet'ül-hakaik* (Quintessential Truths) (1878). These works were seen as apologias for the new Sultan and contained criticisms of his former Young Ottoman associate, Namık Kemal, and his former patron, Midhat Pasha. This earned him the favor of the autocratic Sultan, and indeed Ahmet Midhat held a number of official posts and sinecures throughout his reign. These facts, together with Ahmet Midhat's several spirited defenses of Islam, led to his being characterized as a reactionary by historians and literary critics in the new Republic of Turkey, in line with a new regime that both was aggressively secular and tended to cast the Young Ottoman opposition to Abdülhamid II as its political and intellectual precursor. As a result, for much of the post–World War I twentieth century, Ahmet Midhat's contribution was underestimated in mainstream accounts of the history of Ottoman and Turkish ideas and letters. It is only recently that he has begun to receive some of the attention by scholars that his historical importance surely demands.

5. Niyazi Berkes, *The Development of Secularism in Turkey* (New York: Routledge, 1998), 282.

Index

Ahmet Midhat Efendi (1884–1912), one of the foremost intellectuals of the Ottoman Tanzimat reform era, was a prolific journalist, novelist, playwright, translator, teacher, and social critic. He is typically hailed as the father of the Turkish novel. He was both the head of the first official newspaper of the Ottoman Empire, *Takvim-i Vekayi* (The Calendar of Events), and the founder of the longest running newspaper of the era, *Tercüman-i Hakikat* (Translation of Truth), which ran between 1878 and 1921. He also authored numerous novels and essays on subjects ranging from history to economics to religion. Ahmet Midhat is the subject of renewed interest from cultural, gender, and intellectual historians of the Ottoman Empire and modern Turkey.

Melih Levi graduated from Amherst College with a BA in English Language and Literature in 2015. A native of Istanbul, he is currently working on a series of writings that combine translational poetics and narrative.

Monica M. Ringer teaches Middle Eastern history at Amherst College. Ringer is the author of numerous articles, and two books, *Pious Citizens, Reforming Zoroastrianism in India and Iran* (2011) and *Education, Religion and the Discourse of Cultural Reform in Qajar Iran* (2001). She is currently working on a book project on Islamic modernism.

Printed in the USA
CPSIA information can be obtained
at www.ICGtesting.com
LVHW051018071223
765754LV00004B/338